STAR WARS

THE MANDALORIAN

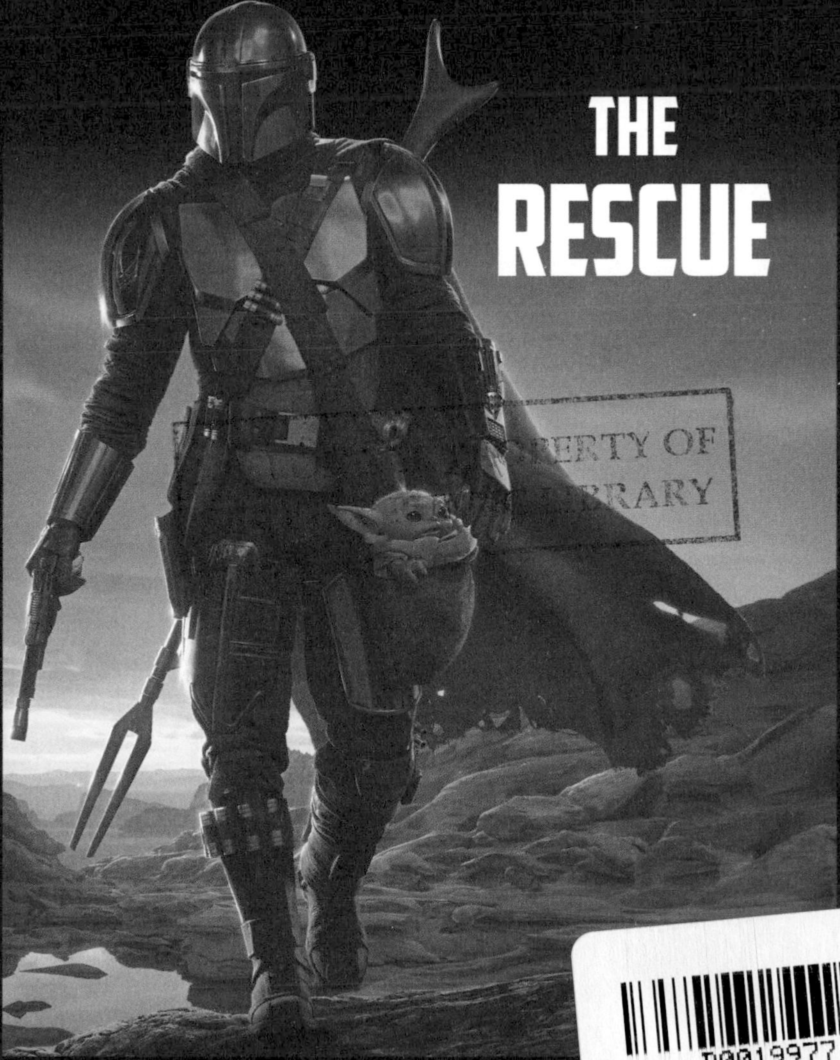
THE RESCUE
ERTY OF
BRARY

RANDOM HOUSE NEW YORK

 Published in the United States by Random House Children's Books, an imprint of Penguin Random House LLC, 1745 Broadway, New York, NY 10019, and in Canada by Penguin Random House Canada Limited, Toronto, in conjunction with Disney Enterprises, Inc. Screen Comix is a trademark of Penguin Random House LLC. Random House and the Random House colophon are registered trademarks of Penguin Random House LLC. ISBN 978-0-7364-4167-4 (trade) ISBN 978-0-7364-4168-1 (ebook)

rhcbooks.com

Printed in the United States of America
10 9 8 7 6 5 4 3 2 1

THE MANDALORIAN ***DIN DJARIN*** HAS RESCUED A CHILD WITH VERY SPECIAL POWERS FROM MOFF GIDEON AND THE REMNANTS OF THE EMPIRE.

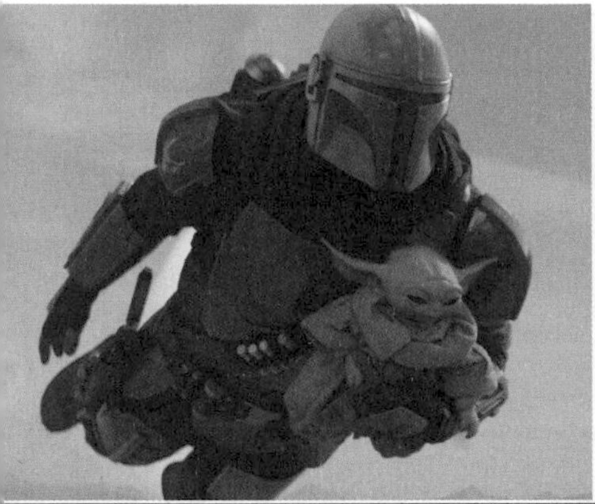

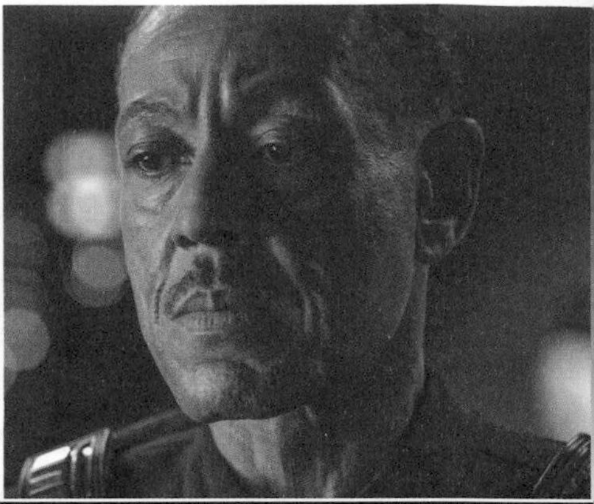

DETERMINED TO REUNITE THE CHILD WITH THE MYSTERIOUS JEDI, DIN DJARIN SETS OFF TO FIND OTHER MANDALORIANS THAT CAN HELP HIM ON HIS QUEST. A GANGSTER NAMED ***GOR KORESH*** REVEALS THAT THERE IS A MANDALORIAN ON TATOOINE.

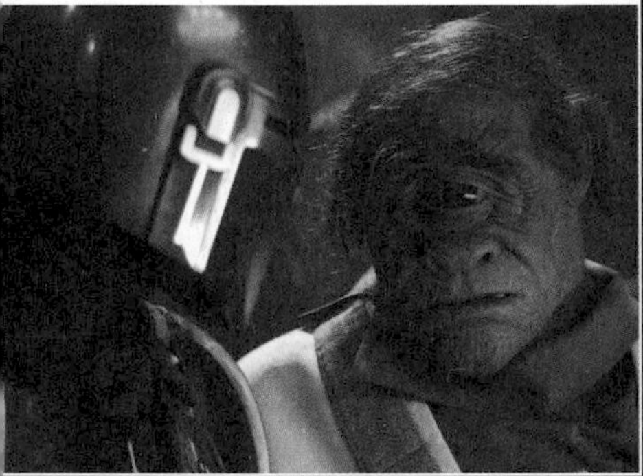

ON TATOOINE, DIN DJARIN MEETS A TOWN MARSHAL NAMED ***COBB VANTH*** WHO WEARS MANDALORIAN ARMOR BOUGHT FROM JAWAS IN THE DESERT. VANTH RELINQUISHES THE ARMOR AFTER THE MANDALORIAN HELPS HIM DESTROY A KRAYT DRAGON TERRORIZING HIS TOWN.

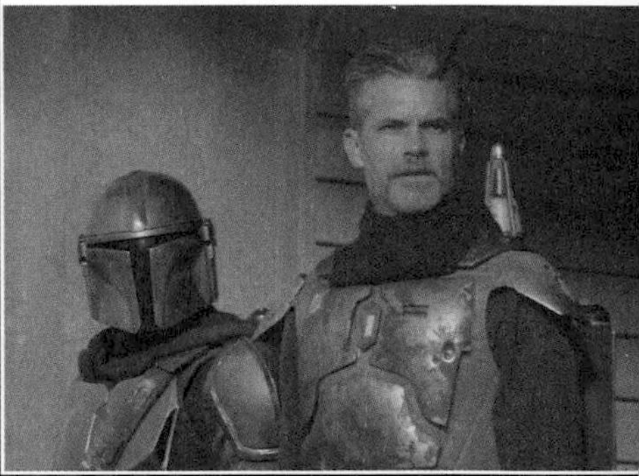

IN EXCHANGE FOR INFORMATION ABOUT THE MANDALORIANS, DIN DJARIN TRANSPORTS A STRANGE FROG-LIKE ALIEN TO THE PLANET TRASK. THERE HE MEETS ***BO-KATAN*** AND TWO OTHER MANDALORIANS. BO-KATAN TELLS DJARIN THAT A JEDI CAN BE FOUND ON THE FOREST PLANET CORVUS.

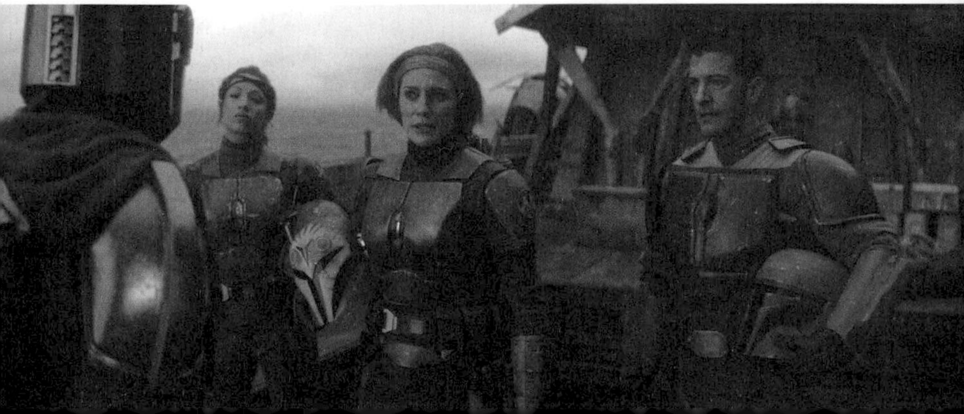

ON CORVUS, JEDI ***AHSOKA TANO*** REVEALS TO THE MANDALORIAN THAT THE CHILD'S NAME IS GROGU. SHE SENDS THEM TO AN ANCIENT TEMPLE ON THE PLANET TYTHON, WHERE GROGU CAN SEND A MESSAGE TO THE JEDI.

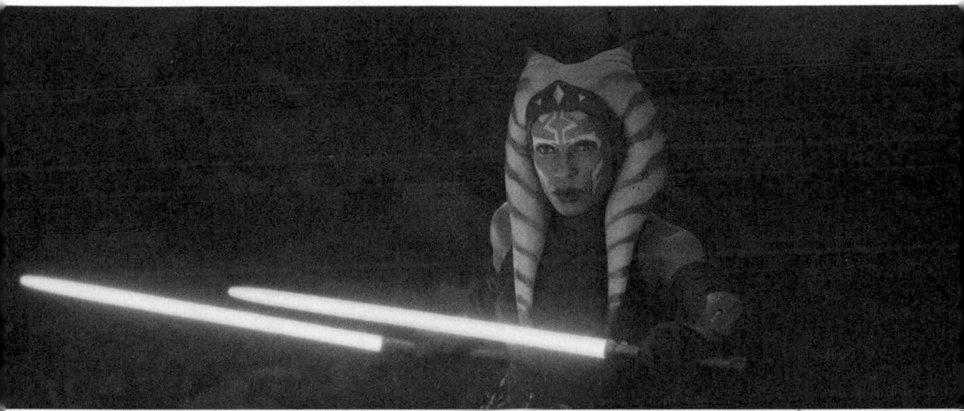

AT THE TEMPLE ON TYTHON, GROGU USES THE FORCE TO REACH OUT TO OTHER JEDI. SUDDENLY, A HEAVILY SCARRED STRANGER APPEARS AND REVEALS THAT HE IS ***BOBA FETT***—THE TRUE OWNER OF THE MANDALORIAN ARMOR.

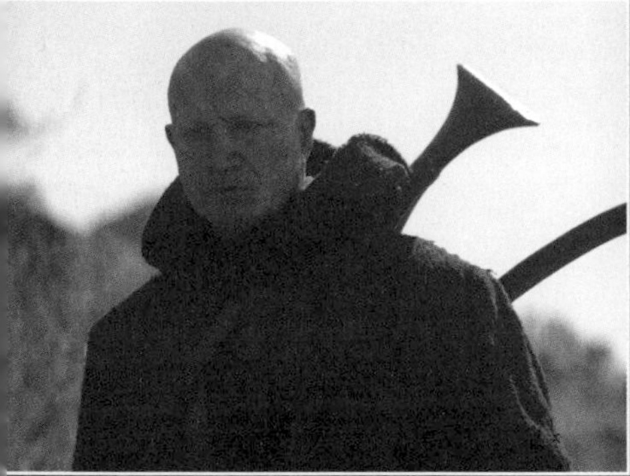

AS FETT AND HIS ALLY FENNEC SHAND TRY TO TAKE THE ARMOR BACK FROM DIN DJARIN, MOFF GIDEON'S ***DARK TROOPERS*** DROP FROM THE SKY AND BLAST OFF WITH GROGU!

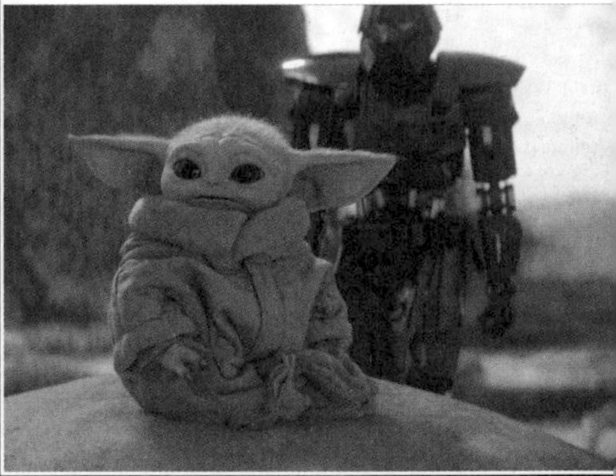

THE MANDALORIAN CALLS UPON THE HELP OF BOBA FETT, FENNEC SHAND, BO-KATAN, KOSKA REEVES, AND FORMER REBEL CARA DUNE TO EMBARK ON A DARING MISSION . . .

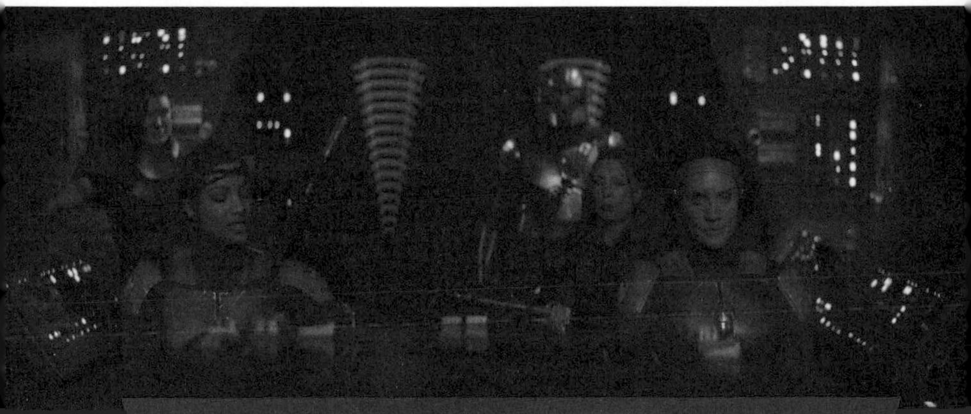

. . . TO RESCUE **GROGU**.

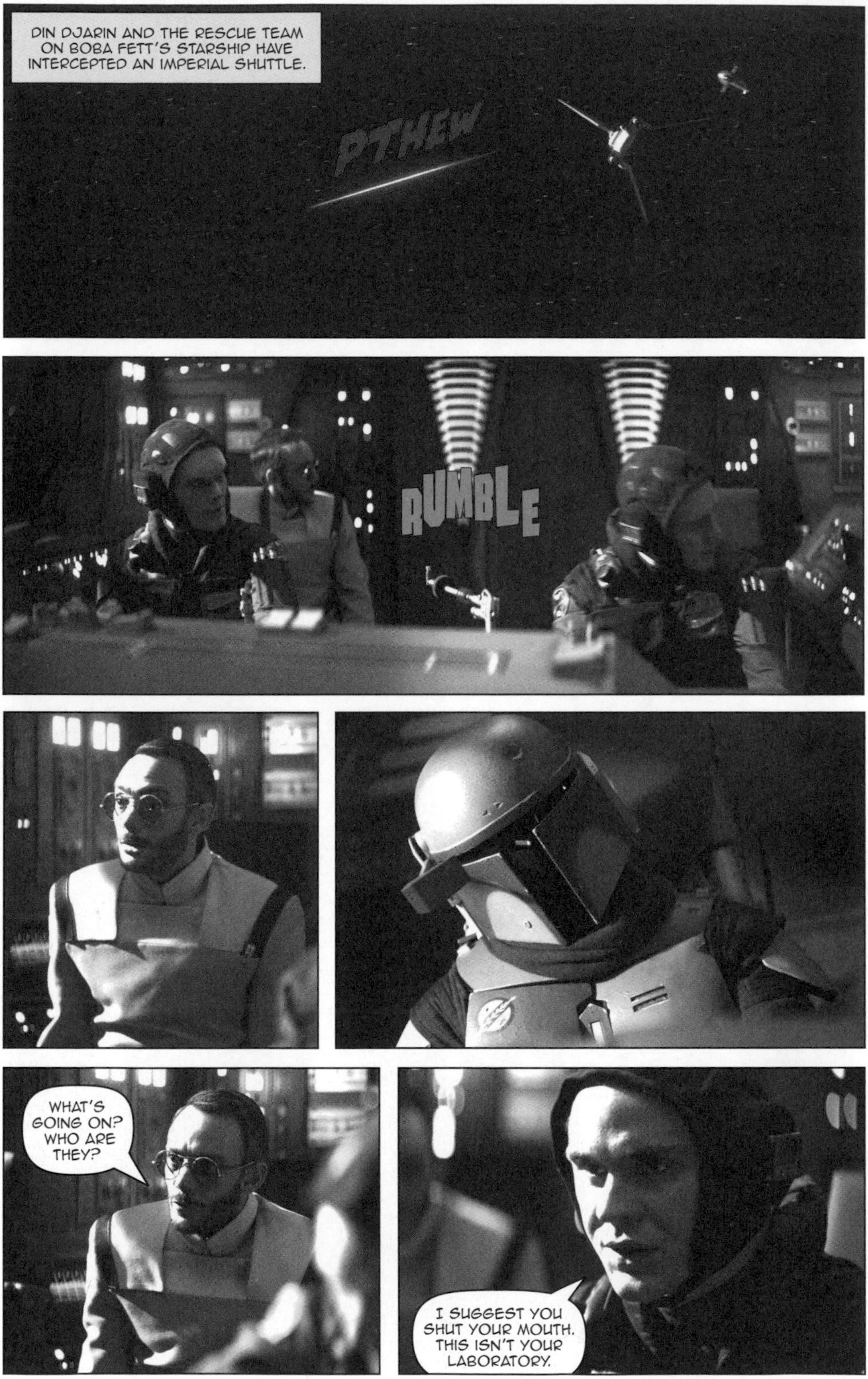
DIN DJARIN AND THE RESCUE TEAM ON BOBA FETT'S STARSHIP HAVE INTERCEPTED AN IMPERIAL SHUTTLE.
PTHEW
RUMBLE
WHAT'S GOING ON? WHO ARE THEY?
I SUGGEST YOU SHUT YOUR MOUTH. THIS ISN'T YOUR LABORATORY.

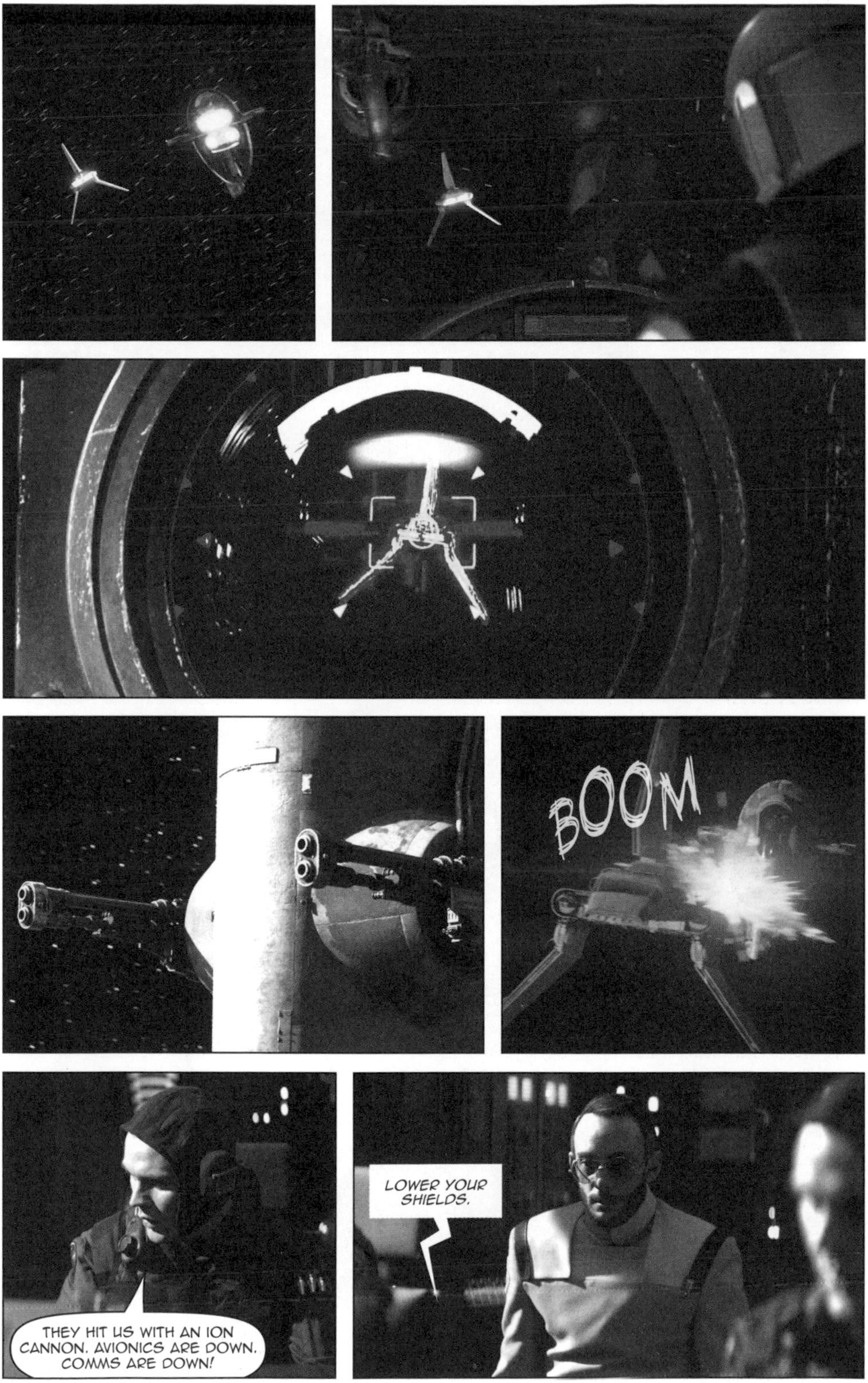
BOOM
THEY HIT US WITH AN ION CANNON. AVIONICS ARE DOWN. COMMS ARE DOWN!
LOWER YOUR SHIELDS.

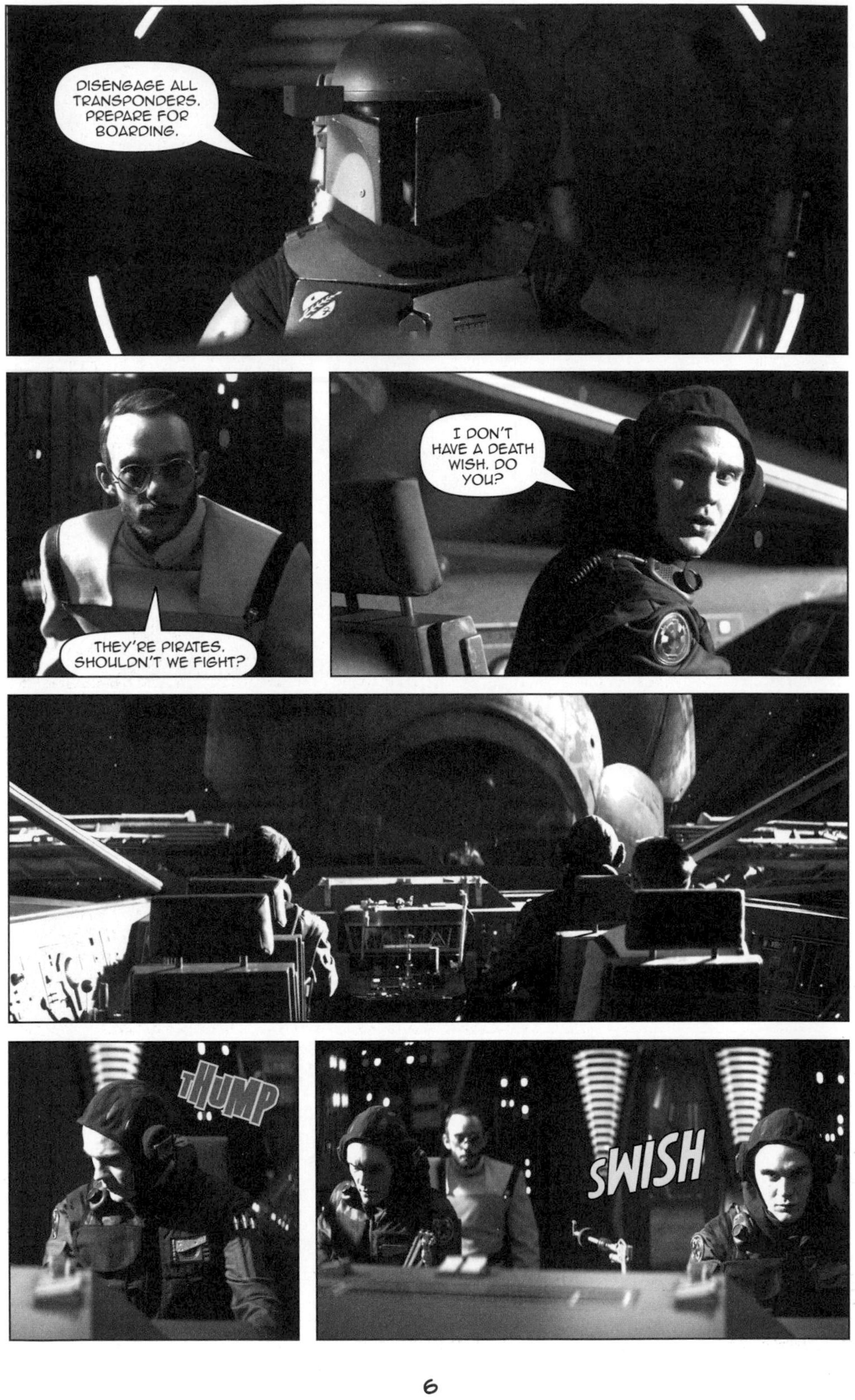
DISENGAGE ALL TRANSPONDERS. PREPARE FOR BOARDING.
THEY'RE PIRATES. SHOULDN'T WE FIGHT?
I DON'T HAVE A DEATH WISH. DO YOU?
tHUMP
SWISH

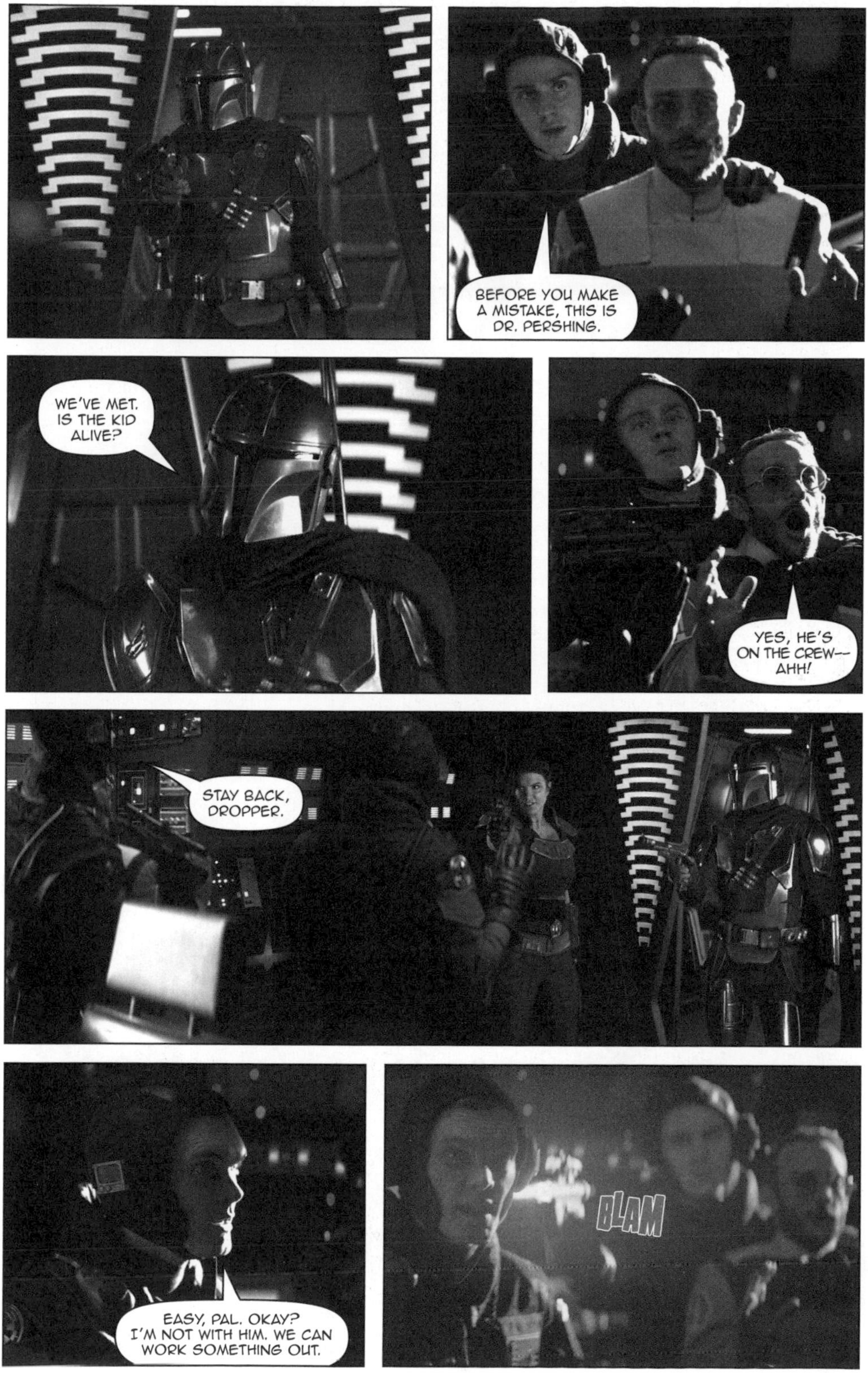
BEFORE YOU MAKE A MISTAKE, THIS IS DR. PERSHING.
WE'VE MET. IS THE KID ALIVE?
YES, HE'S ON THE CREW-- AHH!
STAY BACK, DROPPER.
EASY, PAL. OKAY? I'M NOT WITH HIM. WE CAN WORK SOMETHING OUT.
BLAM

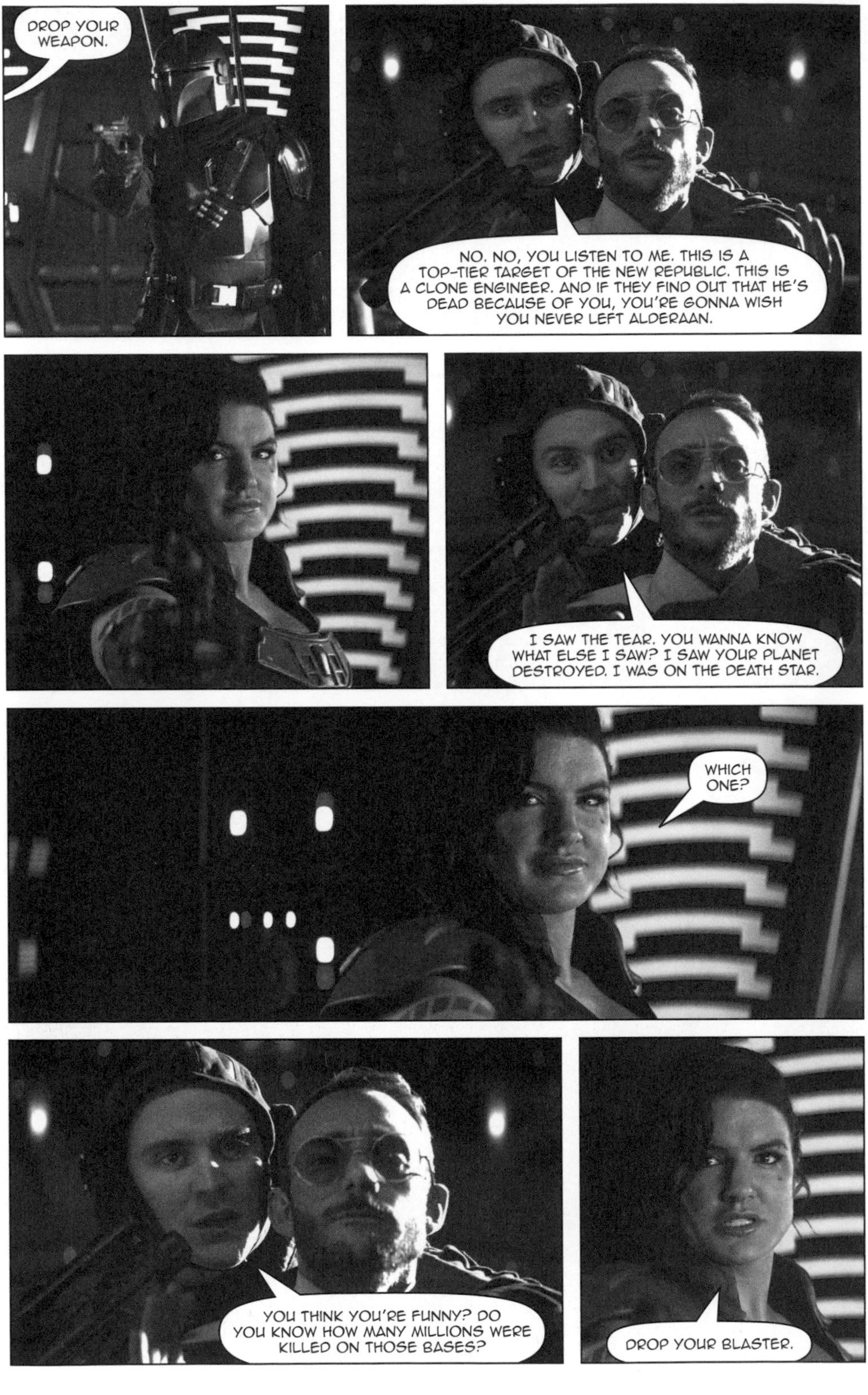
DROP YOUR WEAPON.
NO. NO, YOU LISTEN TO ME. THIS IS A TOP-TIER TARGET OF THE NEW REPUBLIC. THIS IS A CLONE ENGINEER. AND IF THEY FIND OUT THAT HE'S DEAD BECAUSE OF YOU, YOU'RE GONNA WISH YOU NEVER LEFT ALDERAAN.
I SAW THE TEAR. YOU WANNA KNOW WHAT ELSE I SAW? I SAW YOUR PLANET DESTROYED. I WAS ON THE DEATH STAR.
WHICH ONE?
YOU THINK YOU'RE FUNNY? DO YOU KNOW HOW MANY MILLIONS WERE KILLED ON THOSE BASES?
DROP YOUR BLASTER.

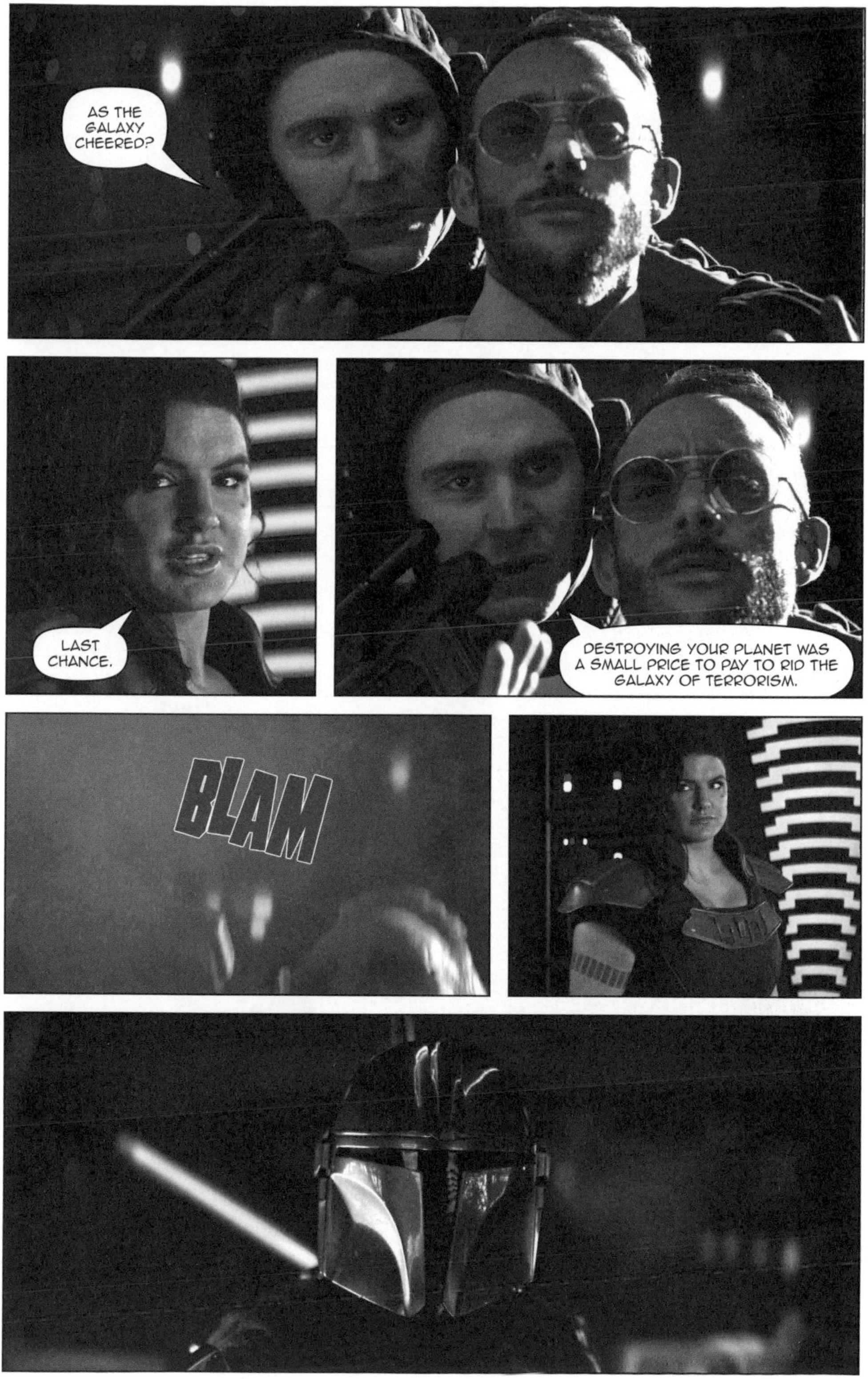
AS THE GALAXY CHEERED?
LAST CHANCE.
DESTROYING YOUR PLANET WAS A SMALL PRICE TO PAY TO RID THE GALAXY OF TERRORISM.
BLAM

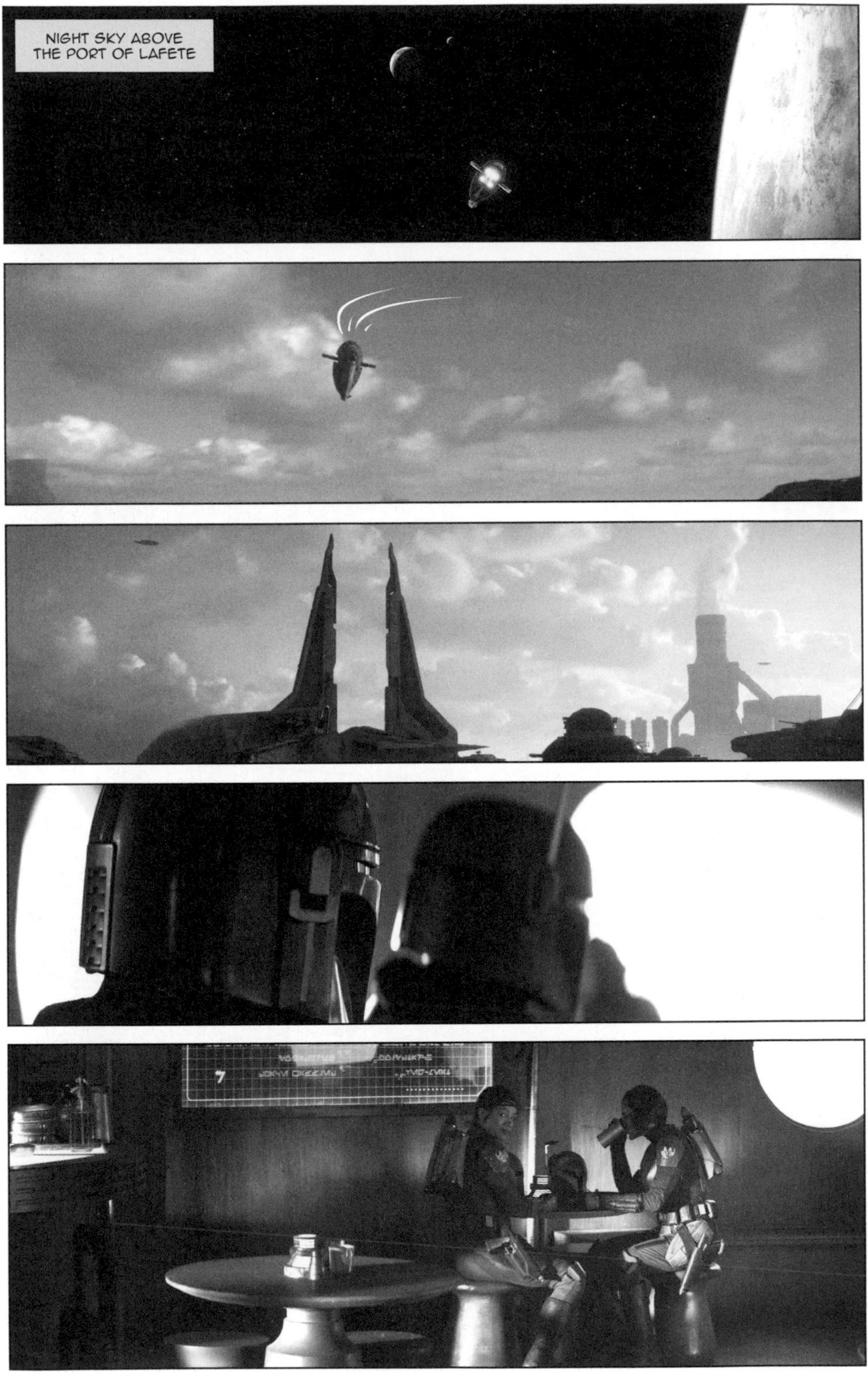
NIGHT SKY ABOVE THE PORT OF LAFETE

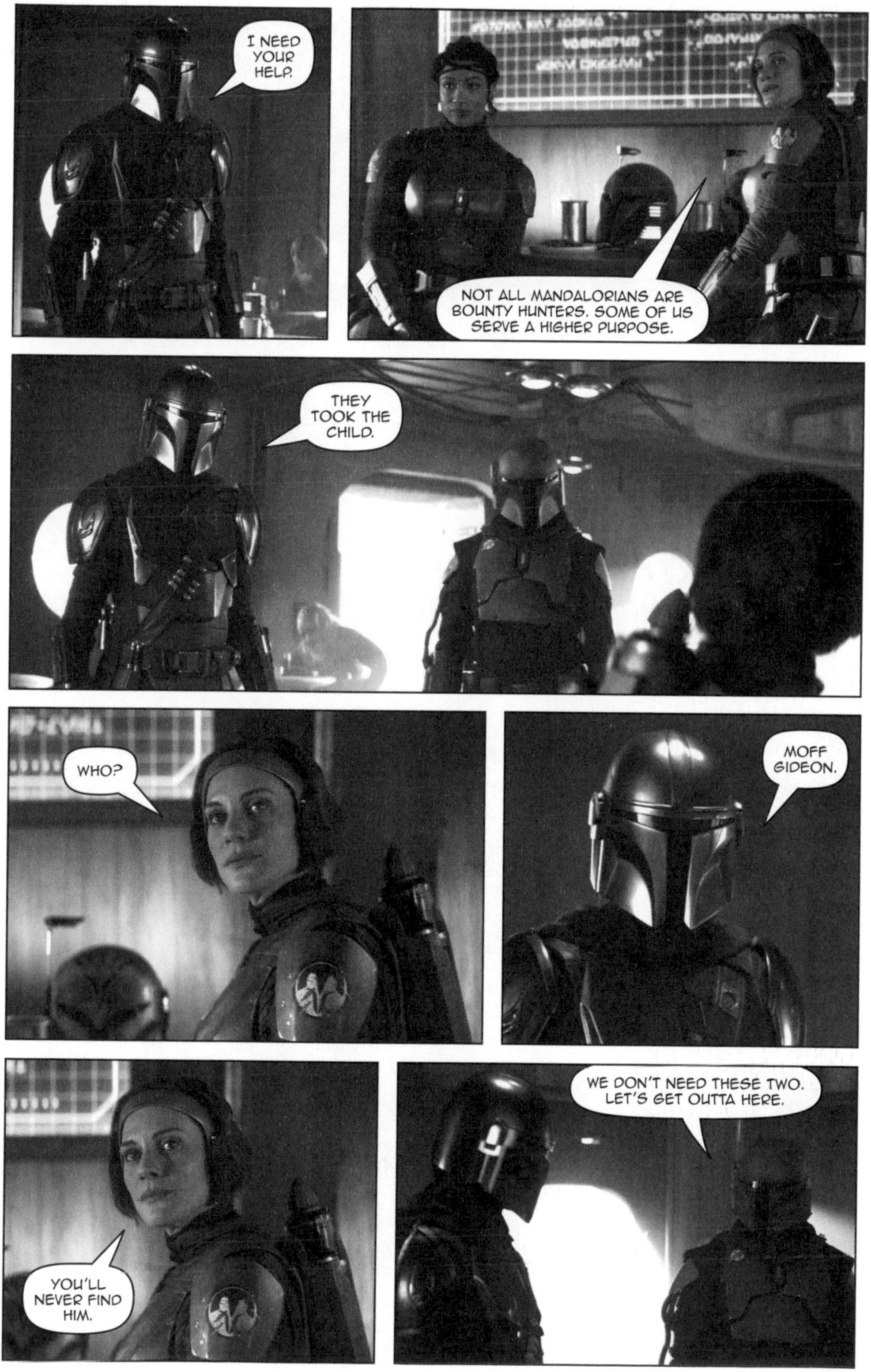
I NEED YOUR HELP.
NOT ALL MANDALORIANS ARE BOUNTY HUNTERS. SOME OF US SERVE A HIGHER PURPOSE.
THEY TOOK THE CHILD.
WHO?
MOFF GIDEON.
YOU'LL NEVER FIND HIM.
WE DON'T NEED THESE TWO. LET'S GET OUTTA HERE.

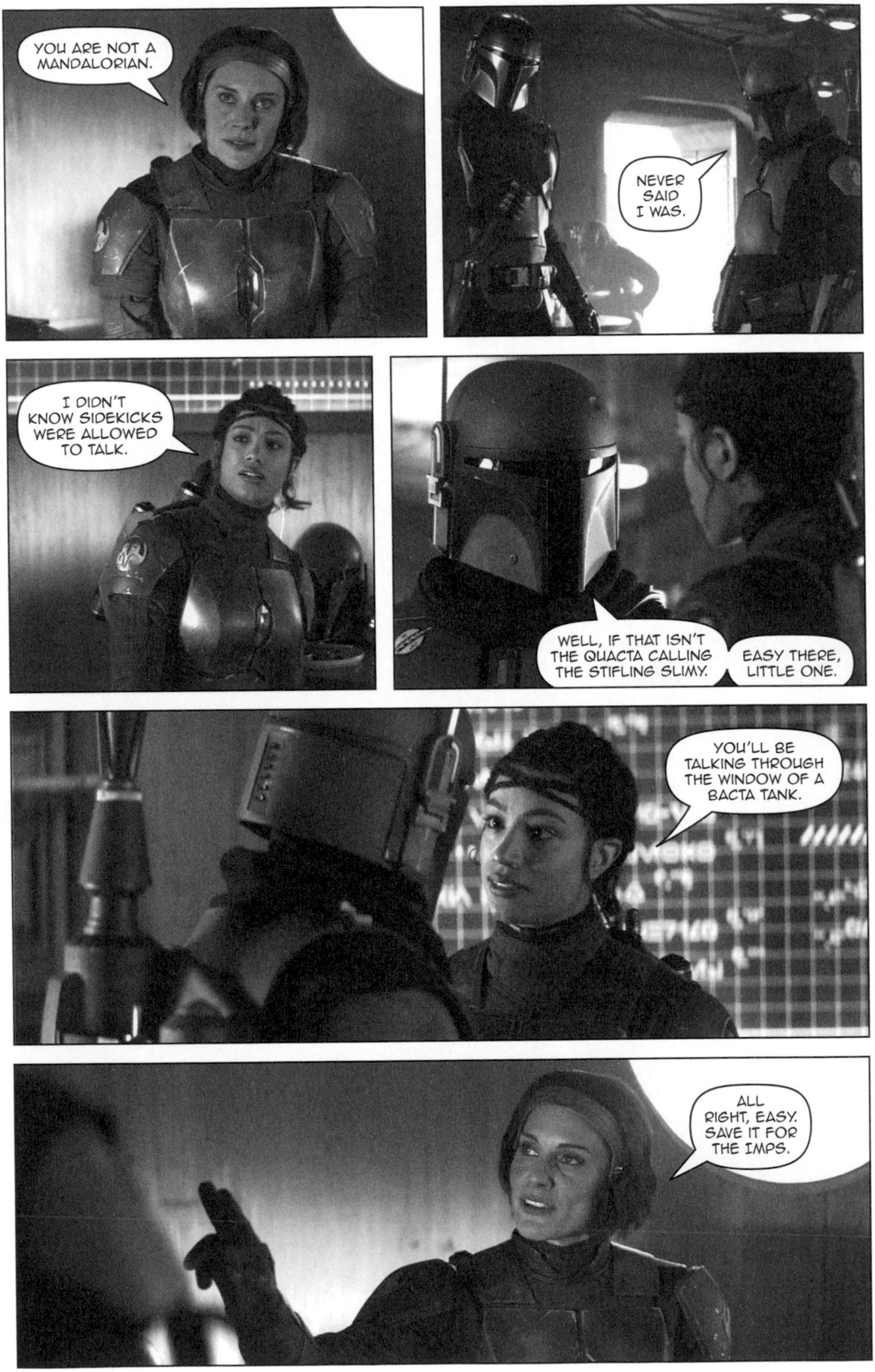
YOU ARE NOT A MANDALORIAN.
NEVER SAID I WAS.
I DIDN'T KNOW SIDEKICKS WERE ALLOWED TO TALK.
WELL, IF THAT ISN'T THE QUACTA CALLING THE STIFLING SLIMY.
EASY THERE, LITTLE ONE.
YOU'LL BE TALKING THROUGH THE WINDOW OF A BACTA TANK.
ALL RIGHT, EASY. SAVE IT FOR THE IMPS.

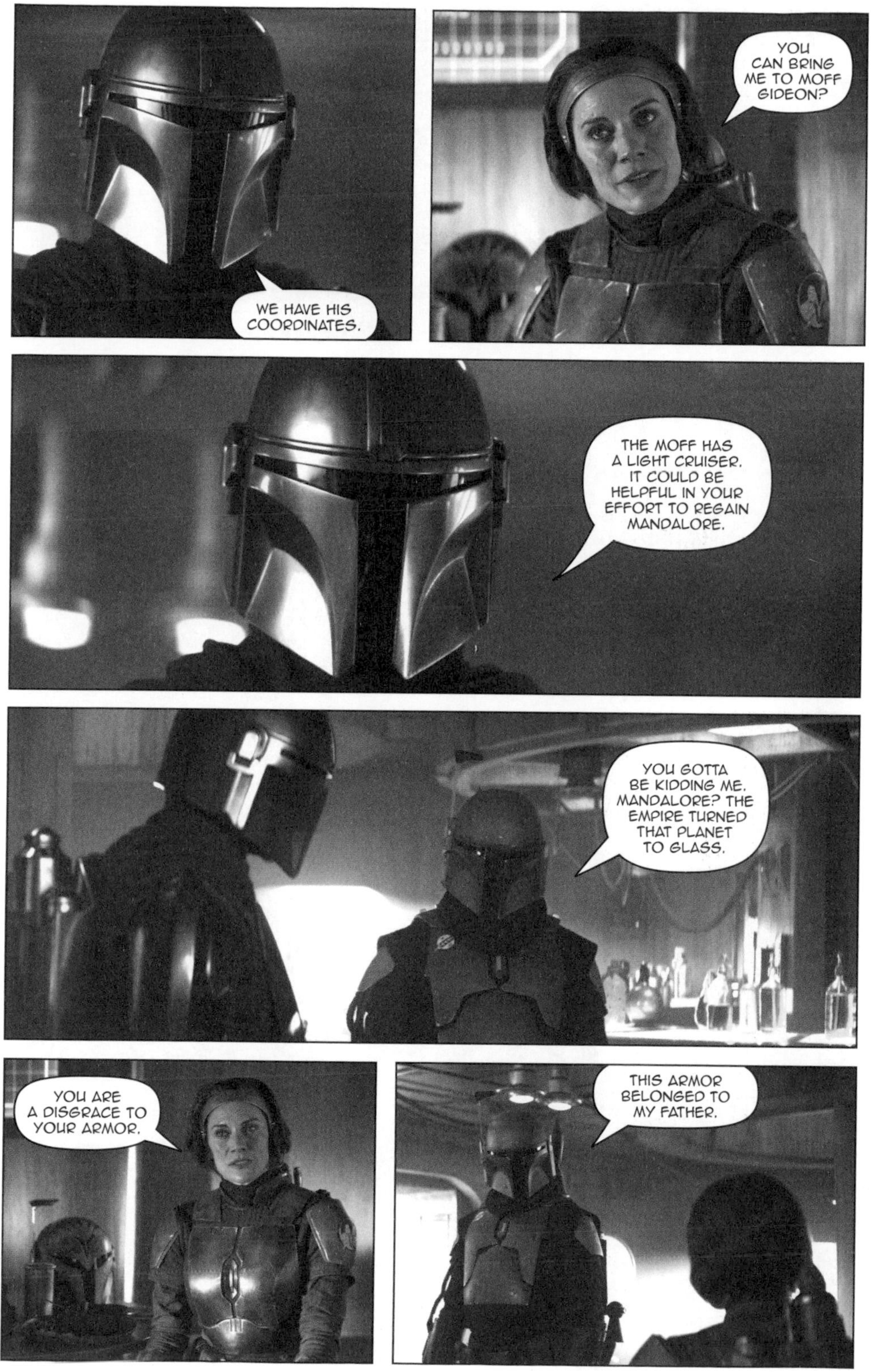
WE HAVE HIS COORDINATES.
YOU CAN BRING ME TO MOFF GIDEON?
THE MOFF HAS A LIGHT CRUISER. IT COULD BE HELPFUL IN YOUR EFFORT TO REGAIN MANDALORE.
YOU GOTTA BE KIDDING ME. MANDALORE? THE EMPIRE TURNED THAT PLANET TO GLASS.
YOU ARE A DISGRACE TO YOUR ARMOR.
THIS ARMOR BELONGED TO MY FATHER.

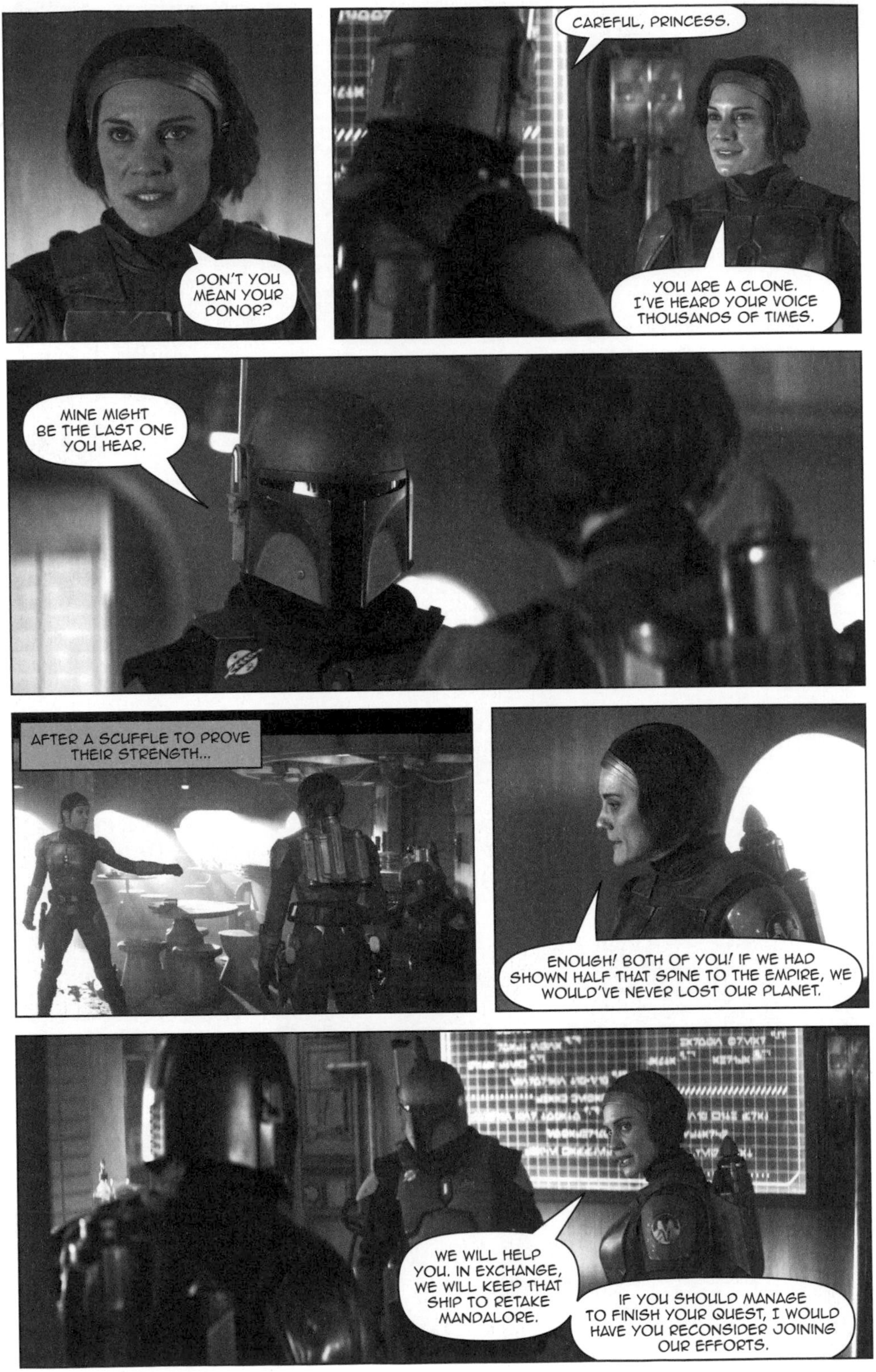
CAREFUL, PRINCESS.
DON'T YOU MEAN YOUR DONOR?
YOU ARE A CLONE. I'VE HEARD YOUR VOICE THOUSANDS OF TIMES.
MINE MIGHT BE THE LAST ONE YOU HEAR.
AFTER A SCUFFLE TO PROVE THEIR STRENGTH...
ENOUGH! BOTH OF YOU! IF WE HAD SHOWN HALF THAT SPINE TO THE EMPIRE, WE WOULD'VE NEVER LOST OUR PLANET.
WE WILL HELP YOU. IN EXCHANGE, WE WILL KEEP THAT SHIP TO RETAKE MANDALORE.
IF YOU SHOULD MANAGE TO FINISH YOUR QUEST, I WOULD HAVE YOU RECONSIDER JOINING OUR EFFORTS.

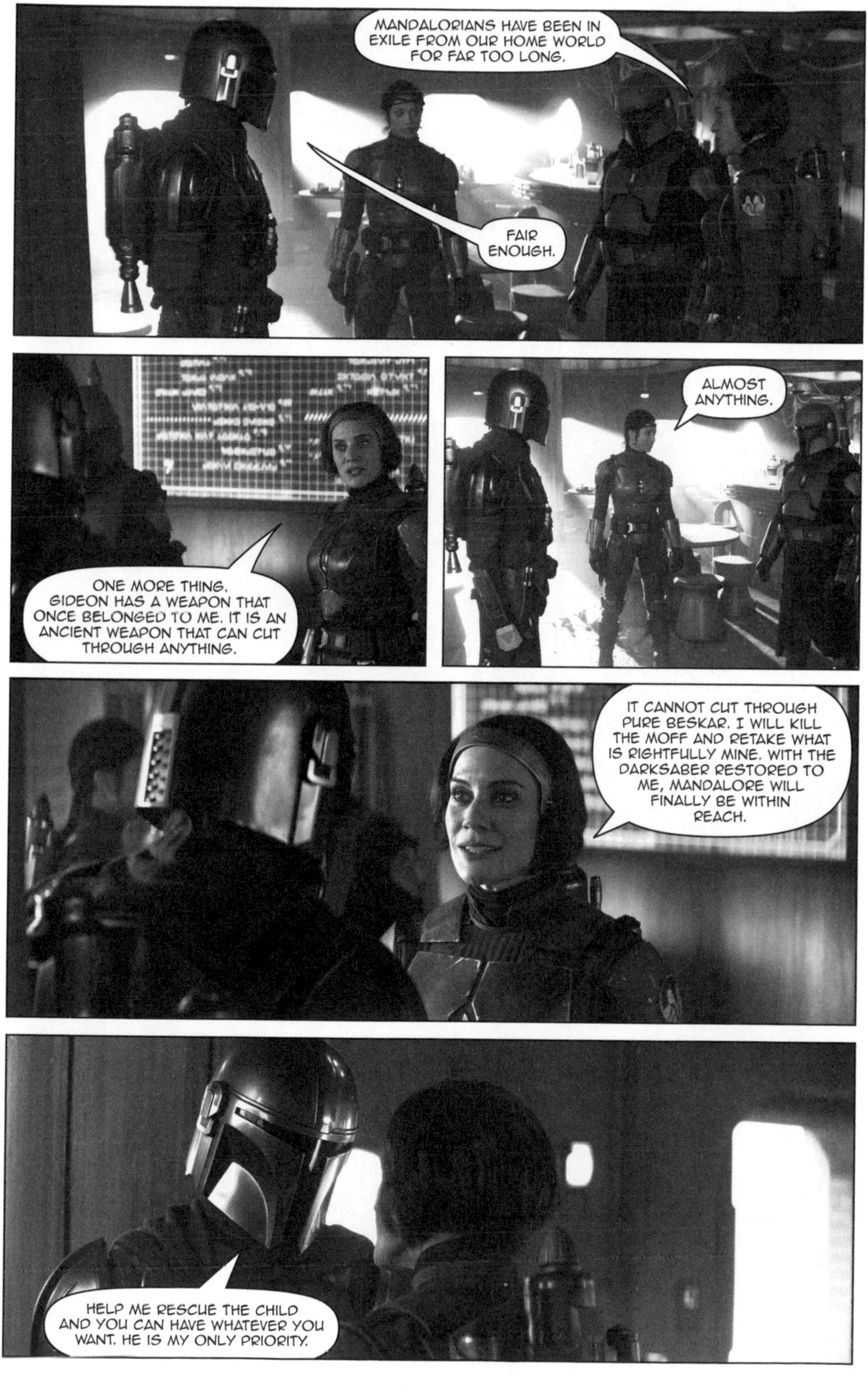
MANDALORIANS HAVE BEEN IN EXILE FROM OUR HOME WORLD FOR FAR TOO LONG.
FAIR ENOUGH.
ONE MORE THING. GIDEON HAS A WEAPON THAT ONCE BELONGED TO ME. IT IS AN ANCIENT WEAPON THAT CAN CUT THROUGH ANYTHING.
ALMOST ANYTHING.
IT CANNOT CUT THROUGH PURE BESKAR. I WILL KILL THE MOFF AND RETAKE WHAT IS RIGHTFULLY MINE. WITH THE DARKSABER RESTORED TO ME, MANDALORE WILL FINALLY BE WITHIN REACH.
HELP ME RESCUE THE CHILD AND YOU CAN HAVE WHATEVER YOU WANT. HE IS MY ONLY PRIORITY.

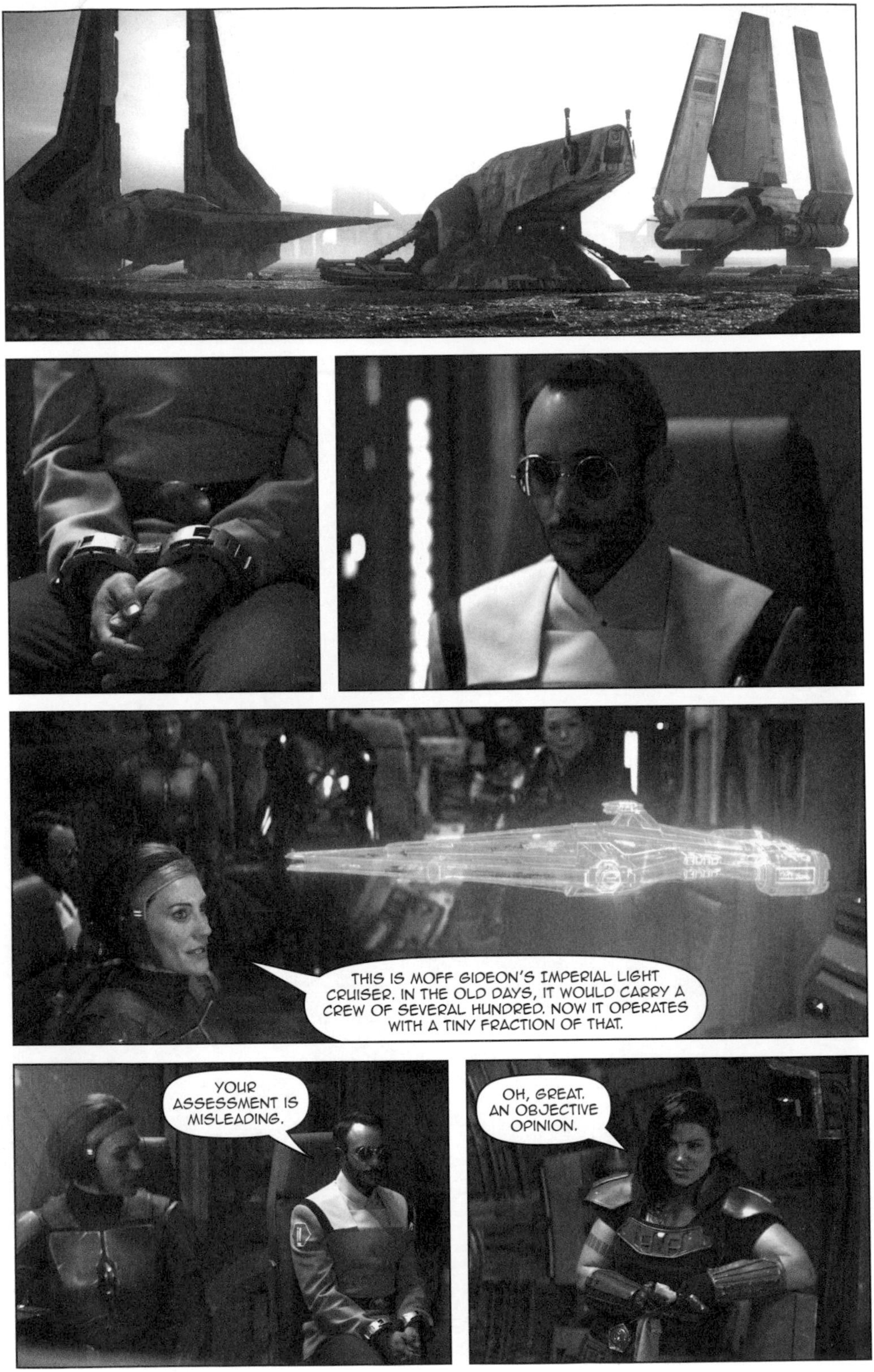
THIS IS MOFF GIDEON'S IMPERIAL LIGHT CRUISER. IN THE OLD DAYS, IT WOULD CARRY A CREW OF SEVERAL HUNDRED. NOW IT OPERATES WITH A TINY FRACTION OF THAT.
YOUR ASSESSMENT IS MISLEADING.
OH, GREAT. AN OBJECTIVE OPINION.

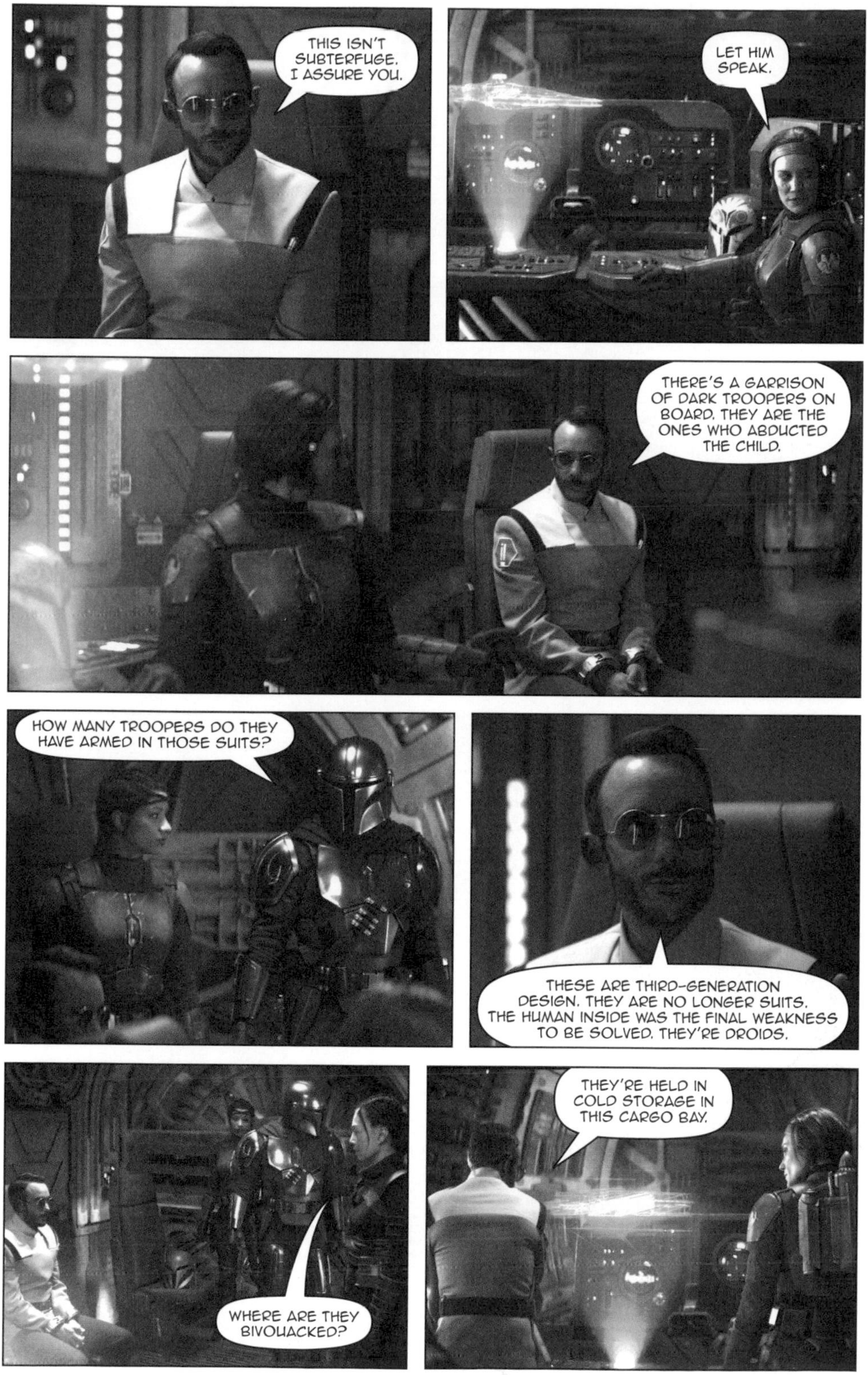
THIS ISN'T SUBTERFUGE. I ASSURE YOU.
LET HIM SPEAK.
THERE'S A GARRISON OF DARK TROOPERS ON BOARD. THEY ARE THE ONES WHO ABDUCTED THE CHILD.
HOW MANY TROOPERS DO THEY HAVE ARMED IN THOSE SUITS?
THESE ARE THIRD-GENERATION DESIGN. THEY ARE NO LONGER SUITS. THE HUMAN INSIDE WAS THE FINAL WEAKNESS TO BE SOLVED. THEY'RE DROIDS.
WHERE ARE THEY BIVOUACKED?
THEY'RE HELD IN COLD STORAGE IN THIS CARGO BAY.

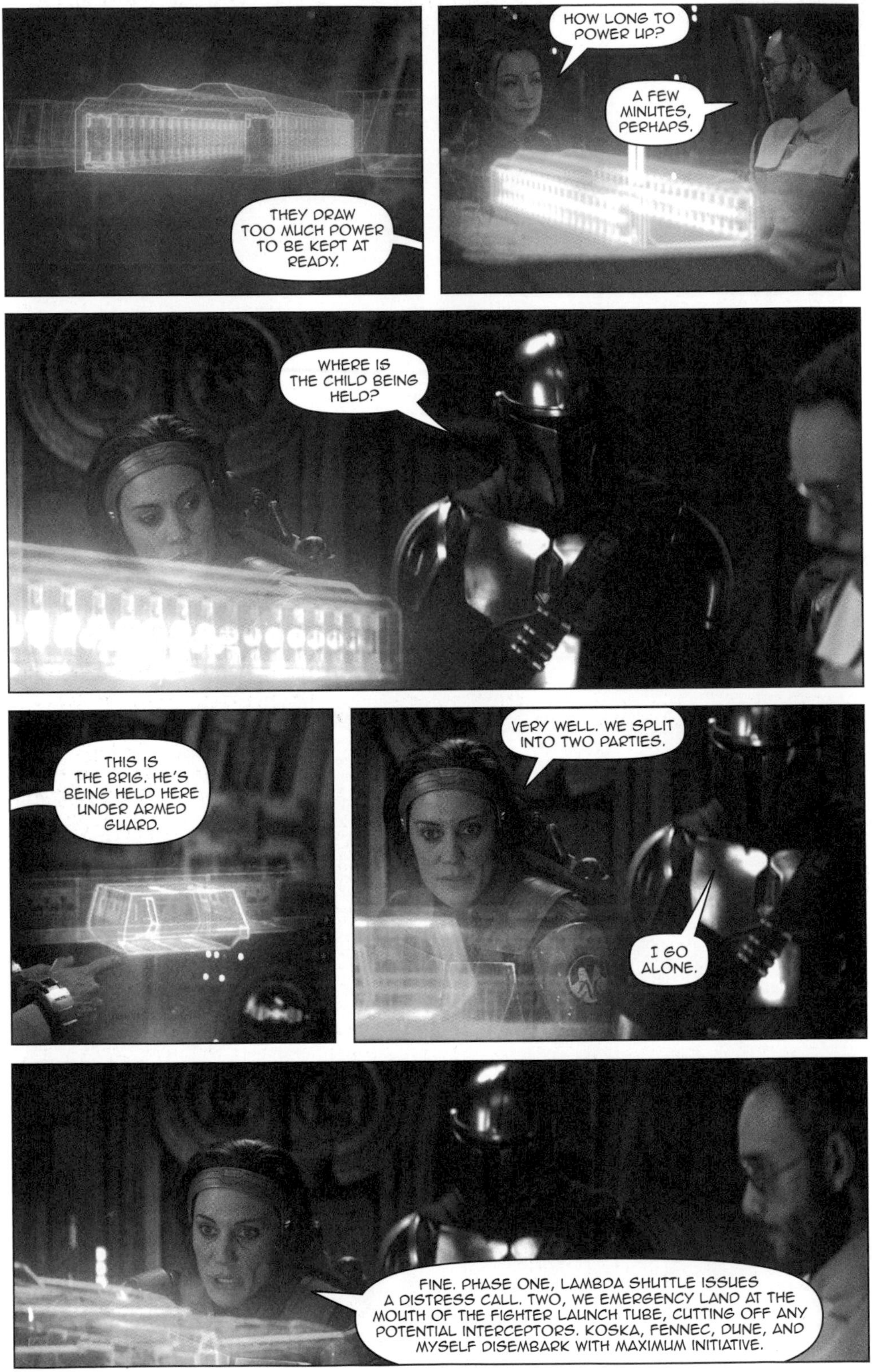
THEY DRAW TOO MUCH POWER TO BE KEPT AT READY.
HOW LONG TO POWER UP?
A FEW MINUTES, PERHAPS.
WHERE IS THE CHILD BEING HELD?
THIS IS THE BRIG. HE'S BEING HELD HERE UNDER ARMED GUARD.
VERY WELL. WE SPLIT INTO TWO PARTIES.
I GO ALONE.
FINE. PHASE ONE, LAMBDA SHUTTLE ISSUES A DISTRESS CALL. TWO, WE EMERGENCY LAND AT THE MOUTH OF THE FIGHTER LAUNCH TUBE, CUTTING OFF ANY POTENTIAL INTERCEPTORS. KOSKA, FENNEC, DUNE, AND MYSELF DISEMBARK WITH MAXIMUM INITIATIVE.

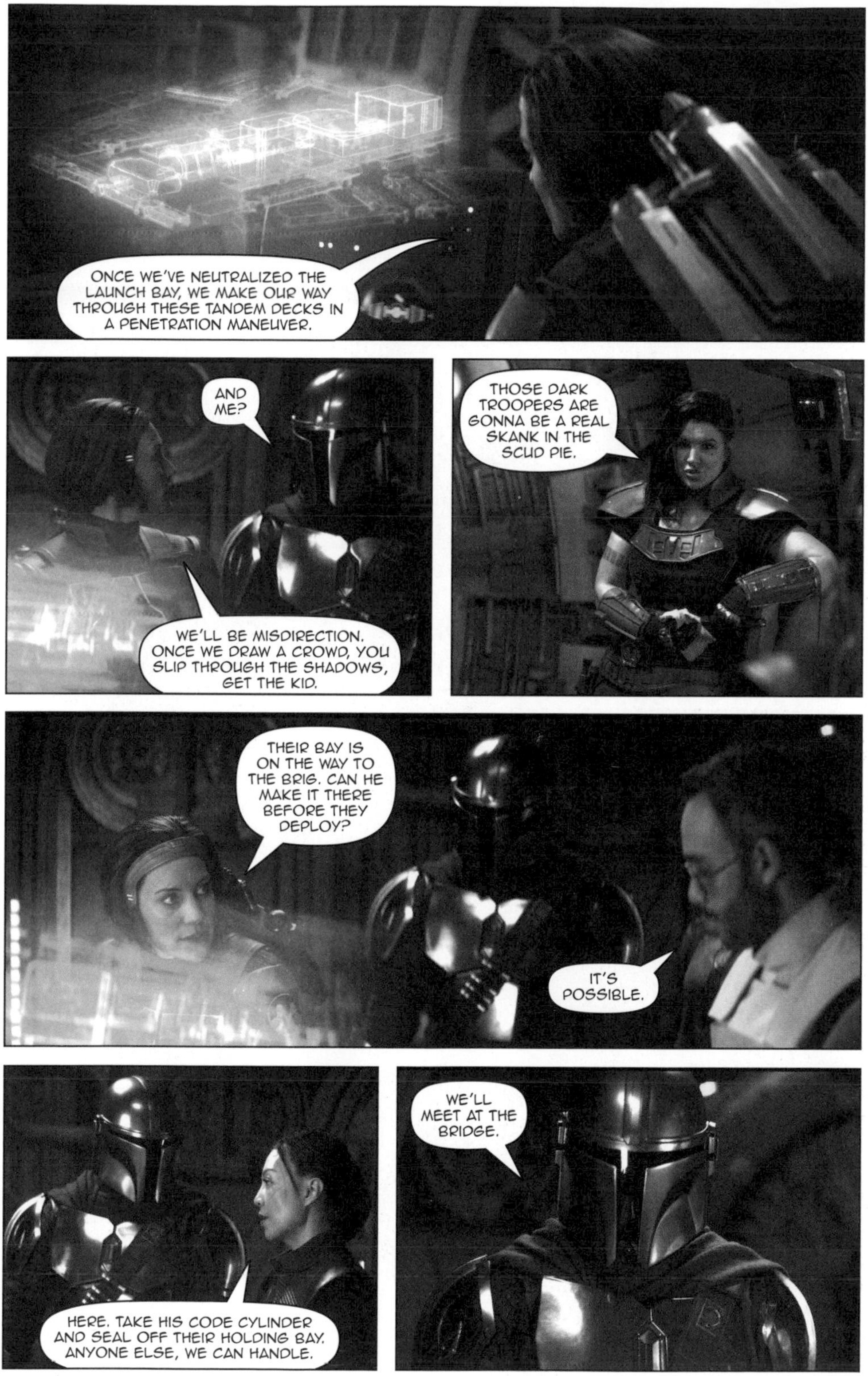
ONCE WE'VE NEUTRALIZED THE LAUNCH BAY, WE MAKE OUR WAY THROUGH THESE TANDEM DECKS IN A PENETRATION MANEUVER.
AND ME?
WE'LL BE MISDIRECTION. ONCE WE DRAW A CROWD, YOU SLIP THROUGH THE SHADOWS, GET THE KID.
THOSE DARK TROOPERS ARE GONNA BE A REAL SKANK IN THE SCUD PIE.
THEIR BAY IS ON THE WAY TO THE BRIG. CAN HE MAKE IT THERE BEFORE THEY DEPLOY?
IT'S POSSIBLE.
HERE. TAKE HIS CODE CYLINDER AND SEAL OFF THEIR HOLDING BAY. ANYONE ELSE, WE CAN HANDLE.
WE'LL MEET AT THE BRIDGE.

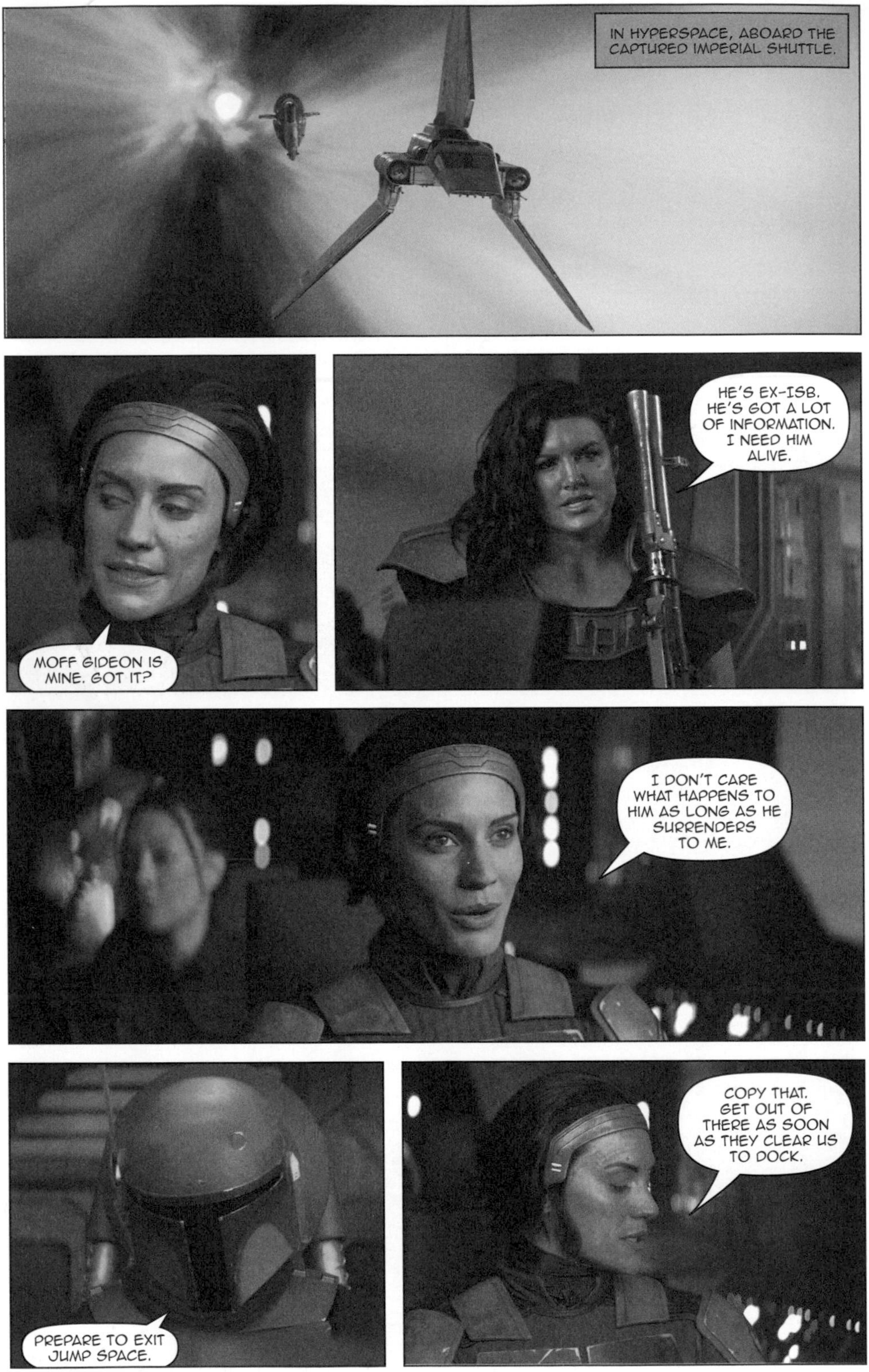
IN HYPERSPACE, ABOARD THE CAPTURED IMPERIAL SHUTTLE.
MOFF GIDEON IS MINE. GOT IT?
HE'S EX-ISB. HE'S GOT A LOT OF INFORMATION. I NEED HIM ALIVE.
I DON'T CARE WHAT HAPPENS TO HIM AS LONG AS HE SURRENDERS TO ME.
PREPARE TO EXIT JUMP SPACE.
COPY THAT. GET OUT OF THERE AS SOON AS THEY CLEAR US TO DOCK.

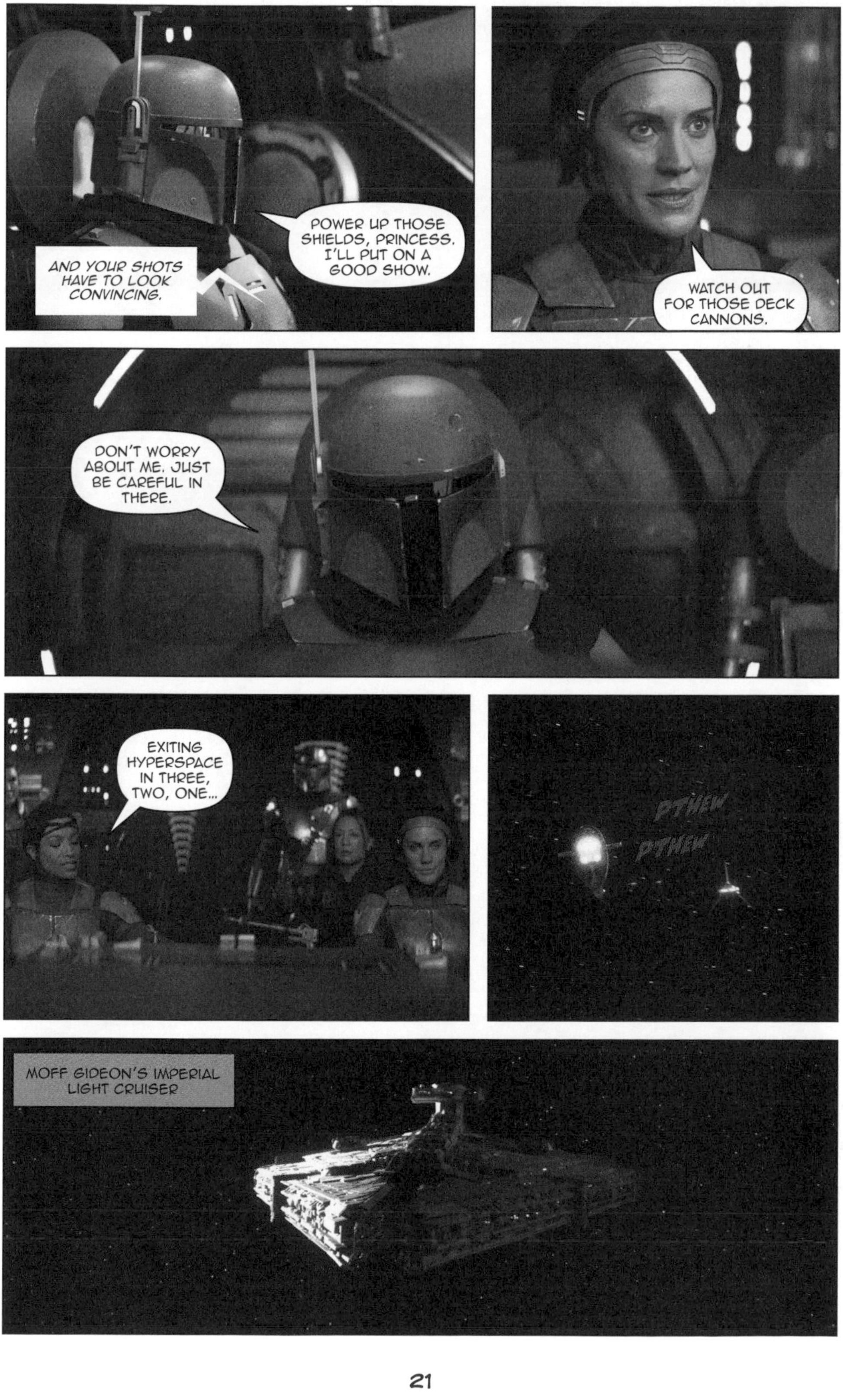
POWER UP THOSE SHIELDS, PRINCESS. I'LL PUT ON A GOOD SHOW.
AND YOUR SHOTS HAVE TO LOOK CONVINCING.
WATCH OUT FOR THOSE DECK CANNONS.
DON'T WORRY ABOUT ME. JUST BE CAREFUL IN THERE.
EXITING HYPERSPACE IN THREE, TWO, ONE...
PTHEW
PTHEW
MOFF GIDEON'S IMPERIAL LIGHT CRUISER

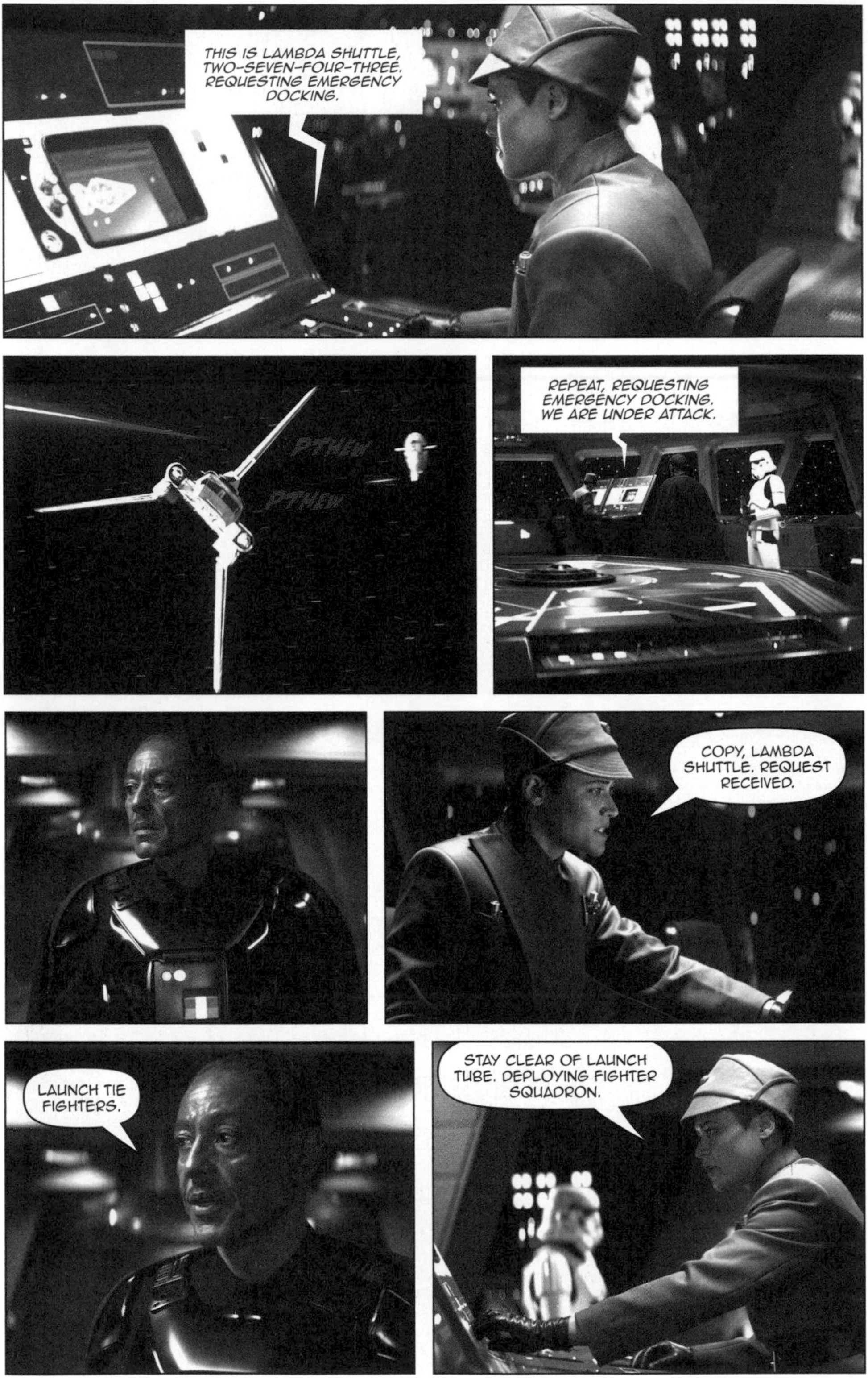
THIS IS LAMBDA SHUTTLE, TWO-SEVEN-FOUR-THREE. REQUESTING EMERGENCY DOCKING.
PTHEW
PTHEW
REPEAT, REQUESTING EMERGENCY DOCKING. WE ARE UNDER ATTACK.
COPY, LAMBDA SHUTTLE. REQUEST RECEIVED.
LAUNCH TIE FIGHTERS.
STAY CLEAR OF LAUNCH TUBE. DEPLOYING FIGHTER SQUADRON.

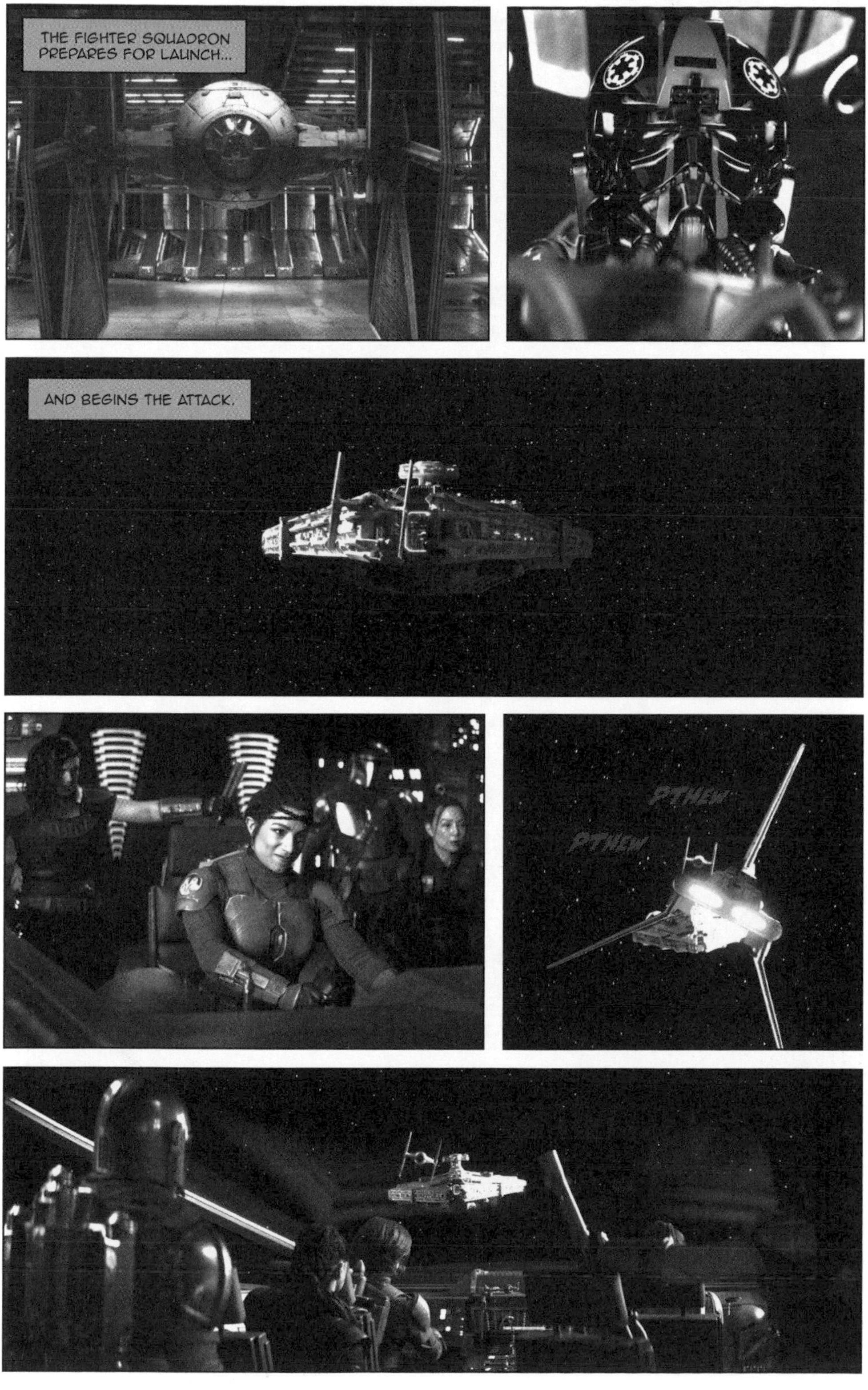
THE FIGHTER SQUADRON PREPARES FOR LAUNCH...
AND BEGINS THE ATTACK.
PTHEW
PTHEW

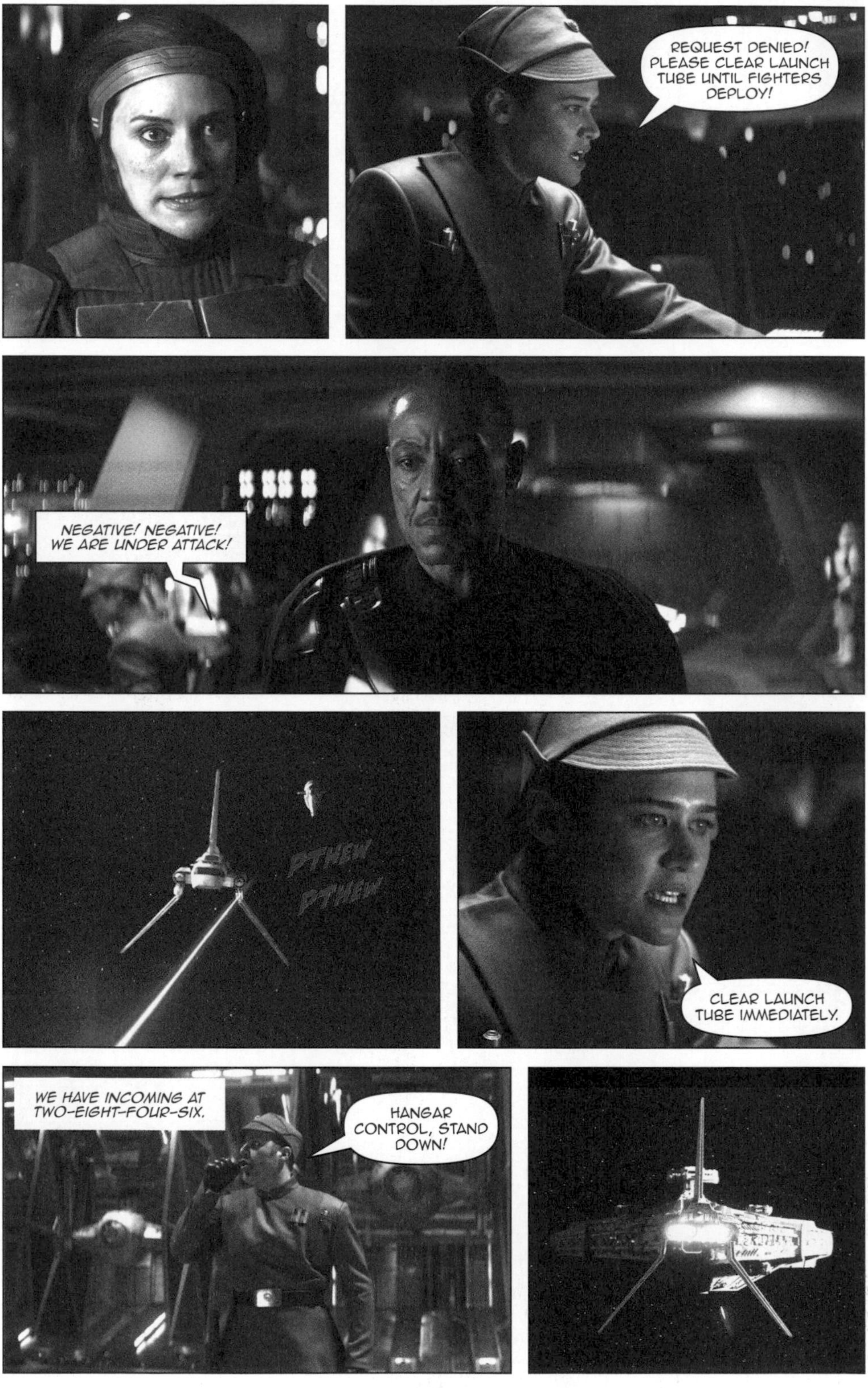
REQUEST DENIED! PLEASE CLEAR LAUNCH TUBE UNTIL FIGHTERS DEPLOY!
NEGATIVE! NEGATIVE! WE ARE UNDER ATTACK!
PTHEW
PTHEW
CLEAR LAUNCH TUBE IMMEDIATELY.
WE HAVE INCOMING AT TWO-EIGHT-FOUR-SIX.
HANGAR CONTROL, STAND DOWN!

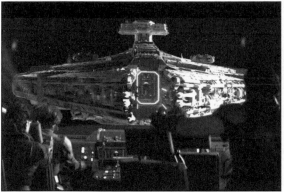

SCREECH

WHAT ARE YOU DOING? GET THAT THING OUT OF HERE!

ZZT

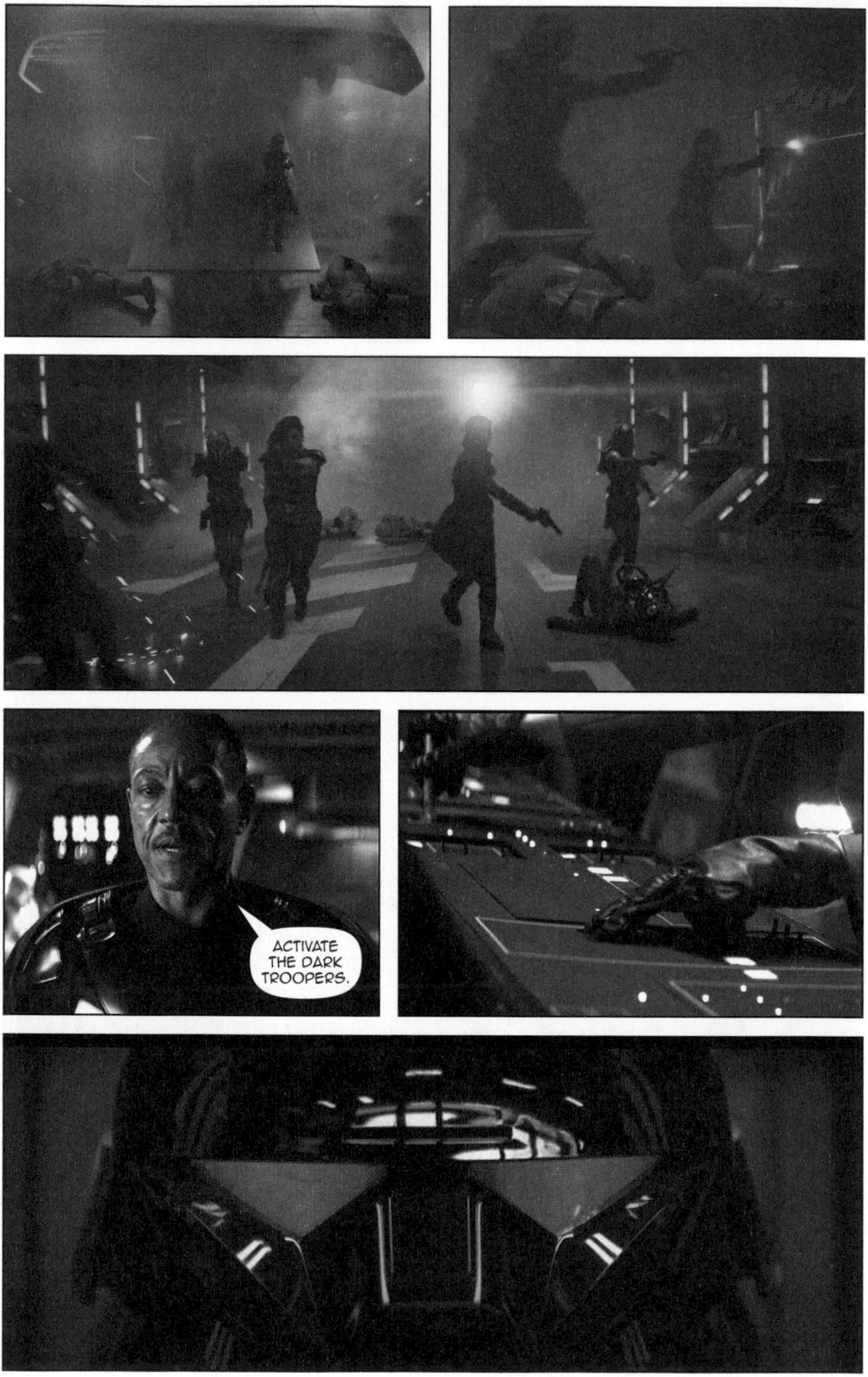
ACTIVATE THE DARK TROOPERS.

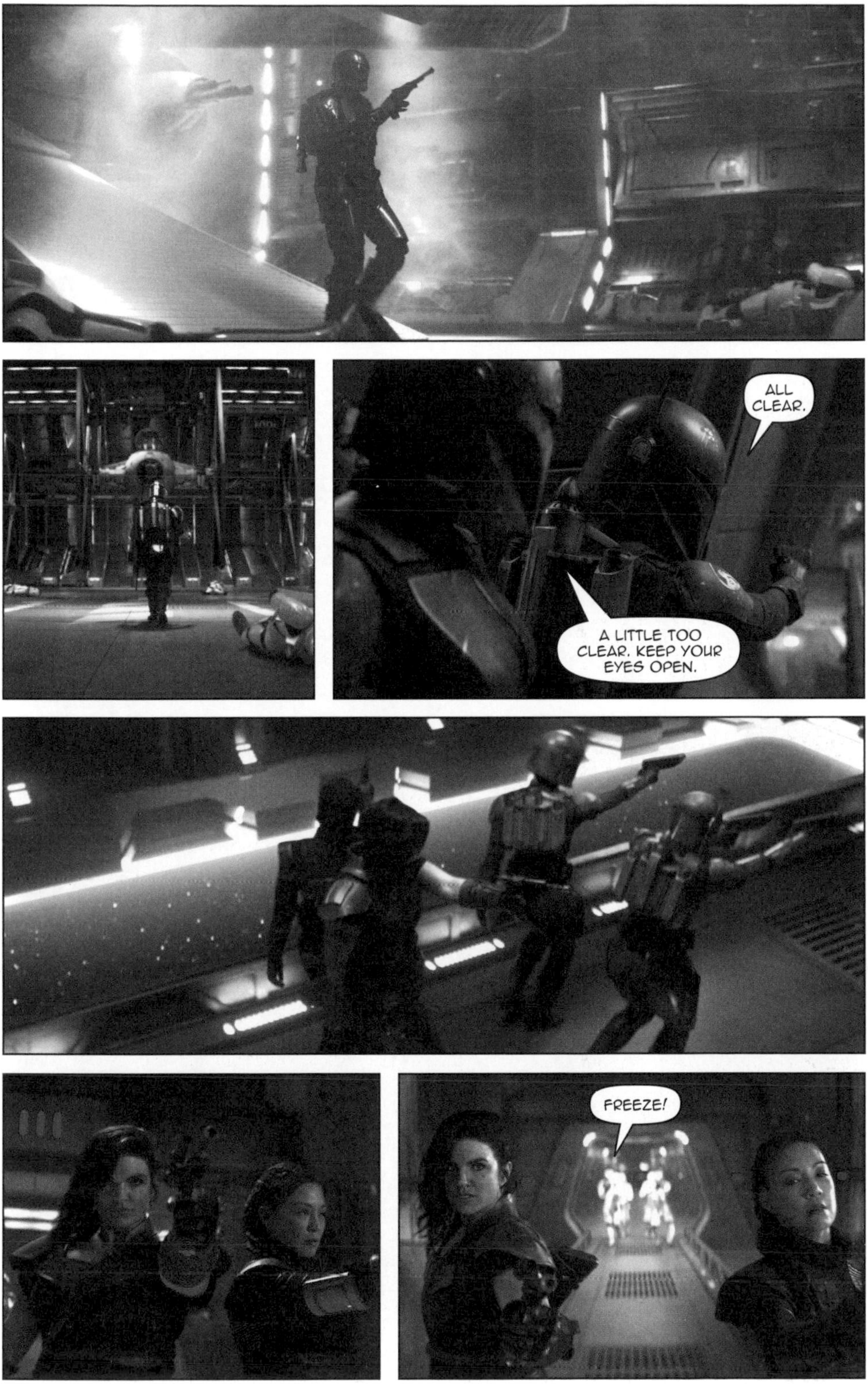
ALL CLEAR.
A LITTLE TOO CLEAR. KEEP YOUR EYES OPEN.
FREEZE!

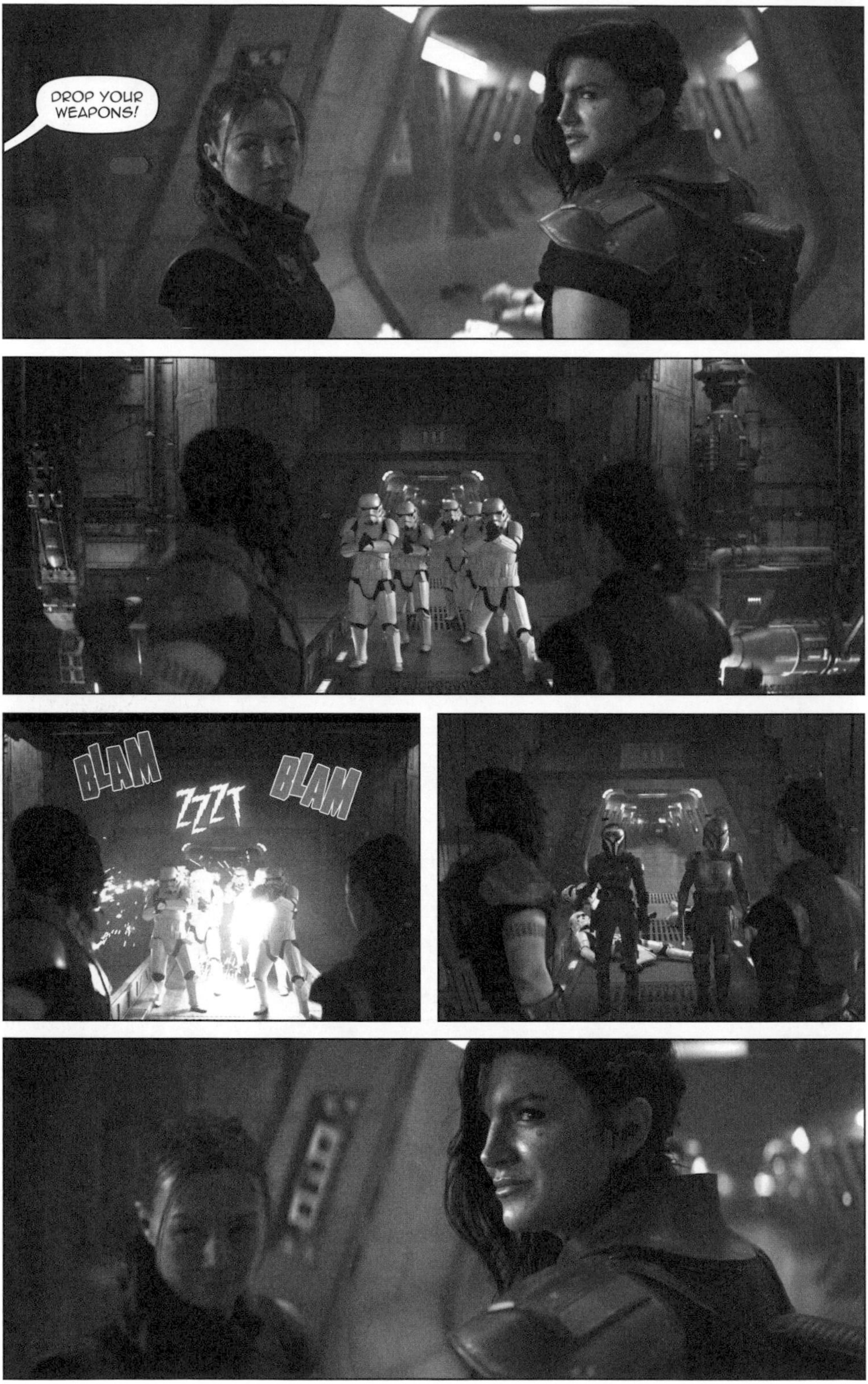
DROP YOUR WEAPONS!
BLAM
ZZZT
BLAM

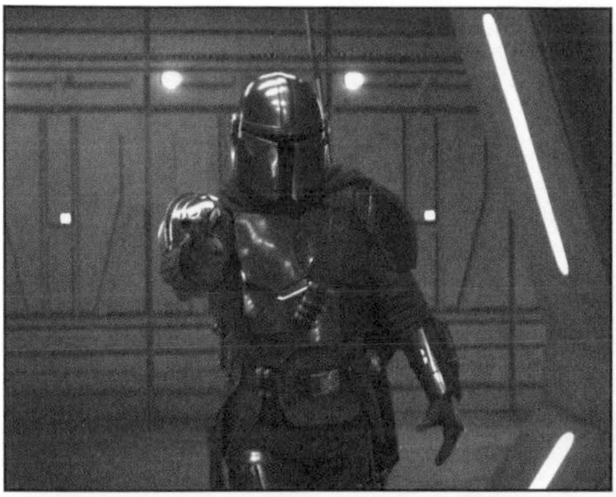

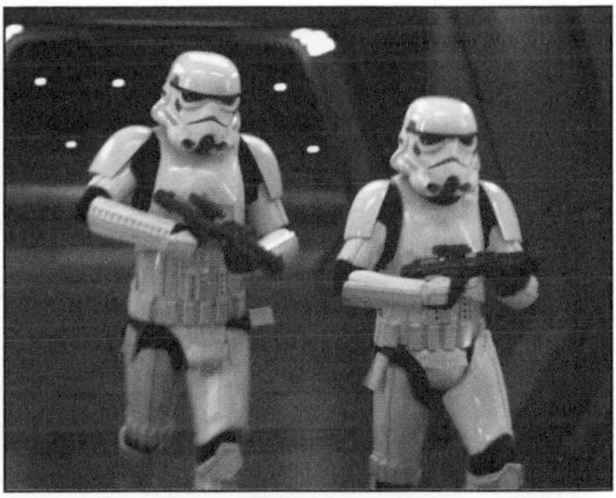

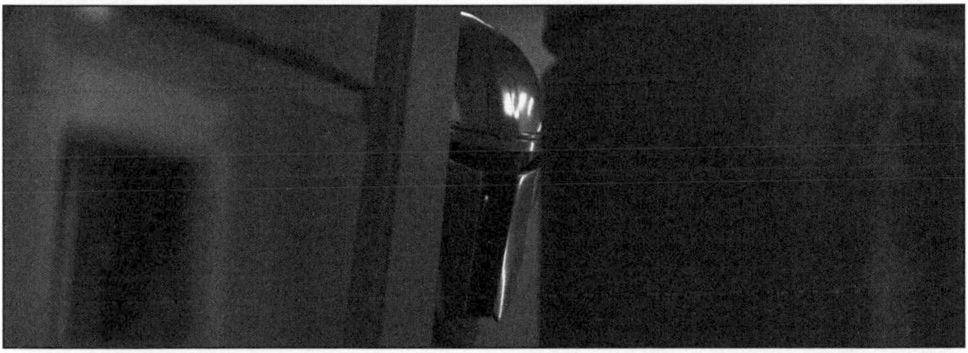

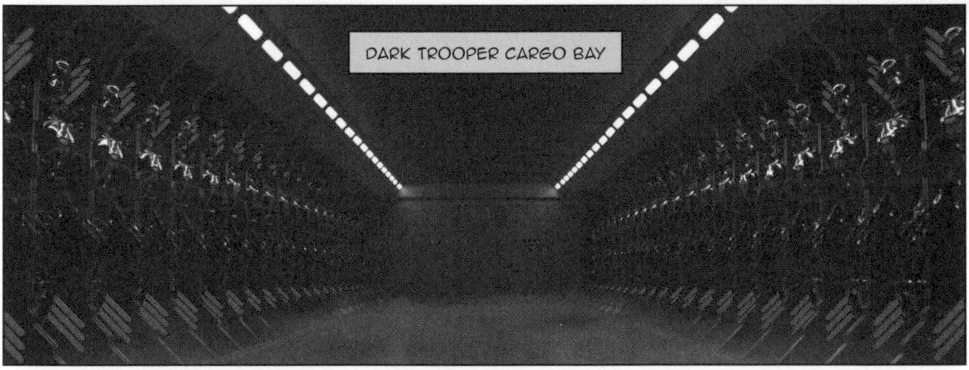
DARK TROOPER CARGO BAY

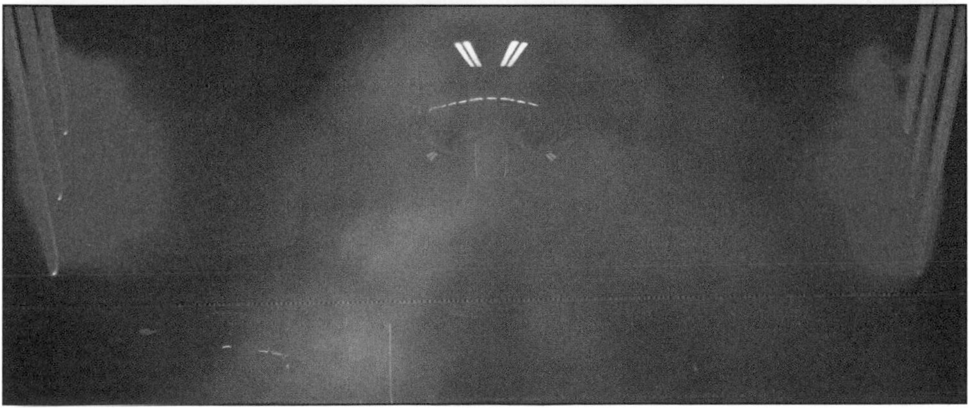

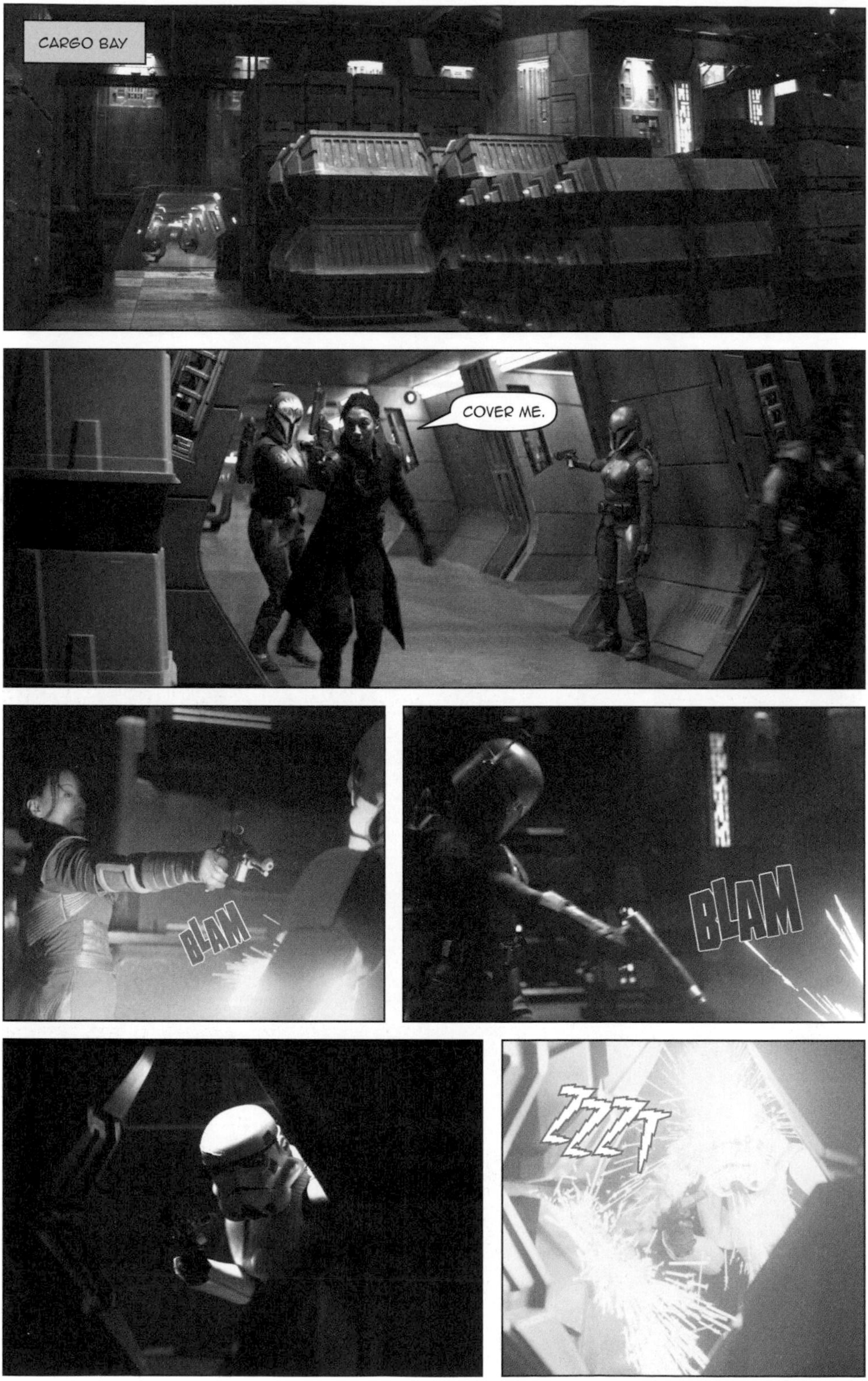
CARGO BAY
COVER ME.
BLAM
BLAM
ZZZT

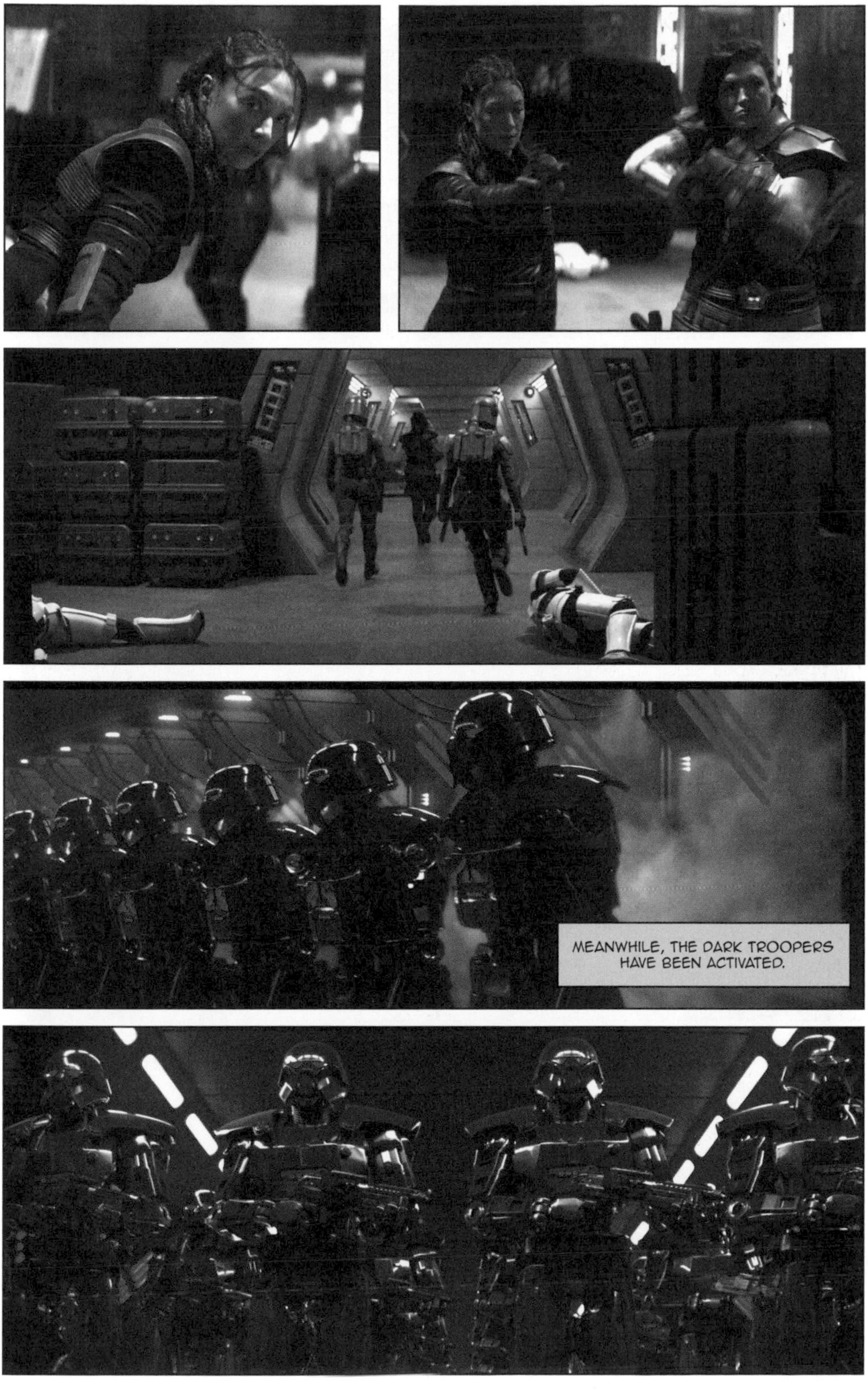
MEANWHILE, THE DARK TROOPERS HAVE BEEN ACTIVATED.

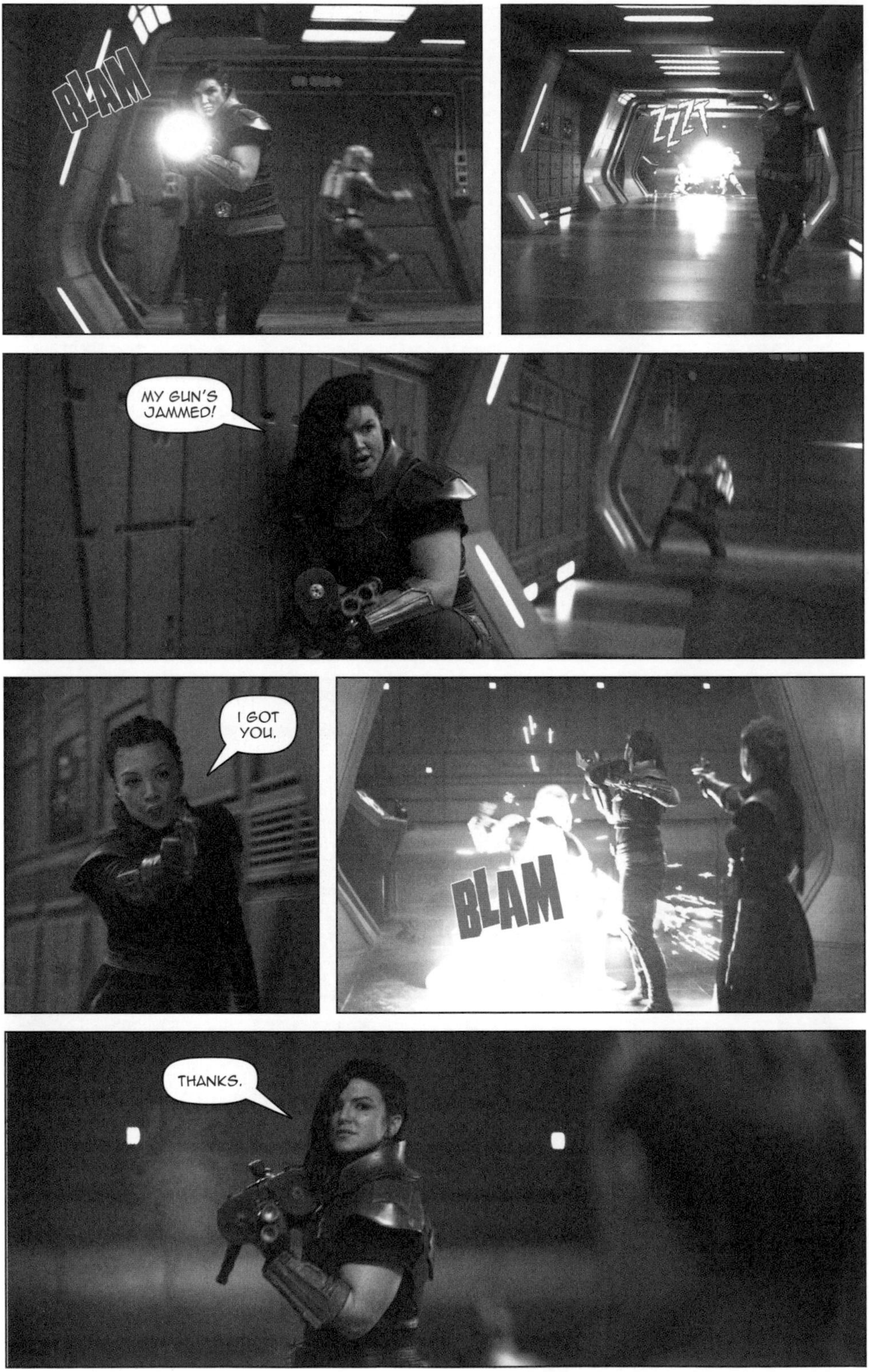
BLAM
ZZZT
MY GUN'S JAMMED!
I GOT YOU.
BLAM
THANKS.

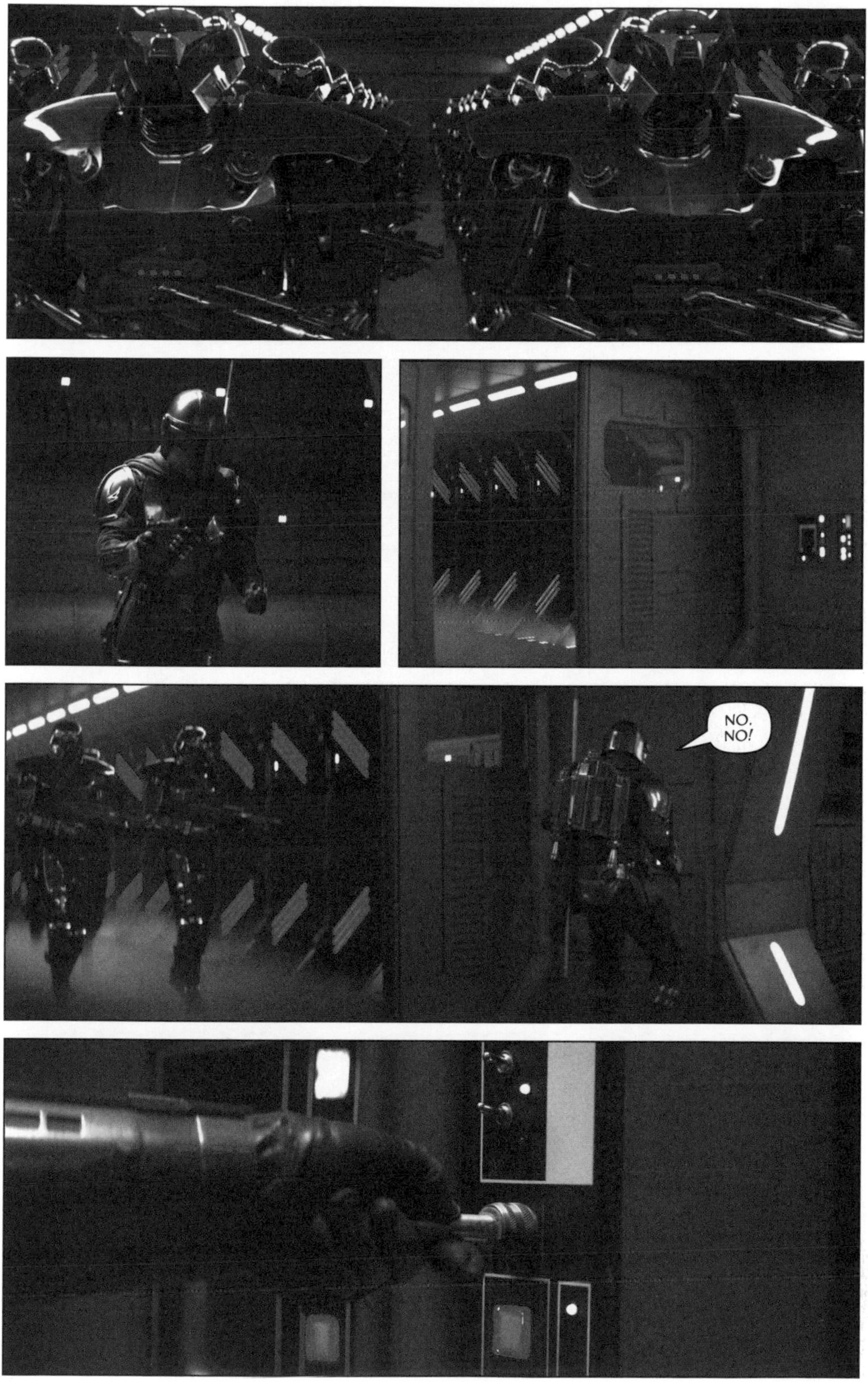
NO, NO!

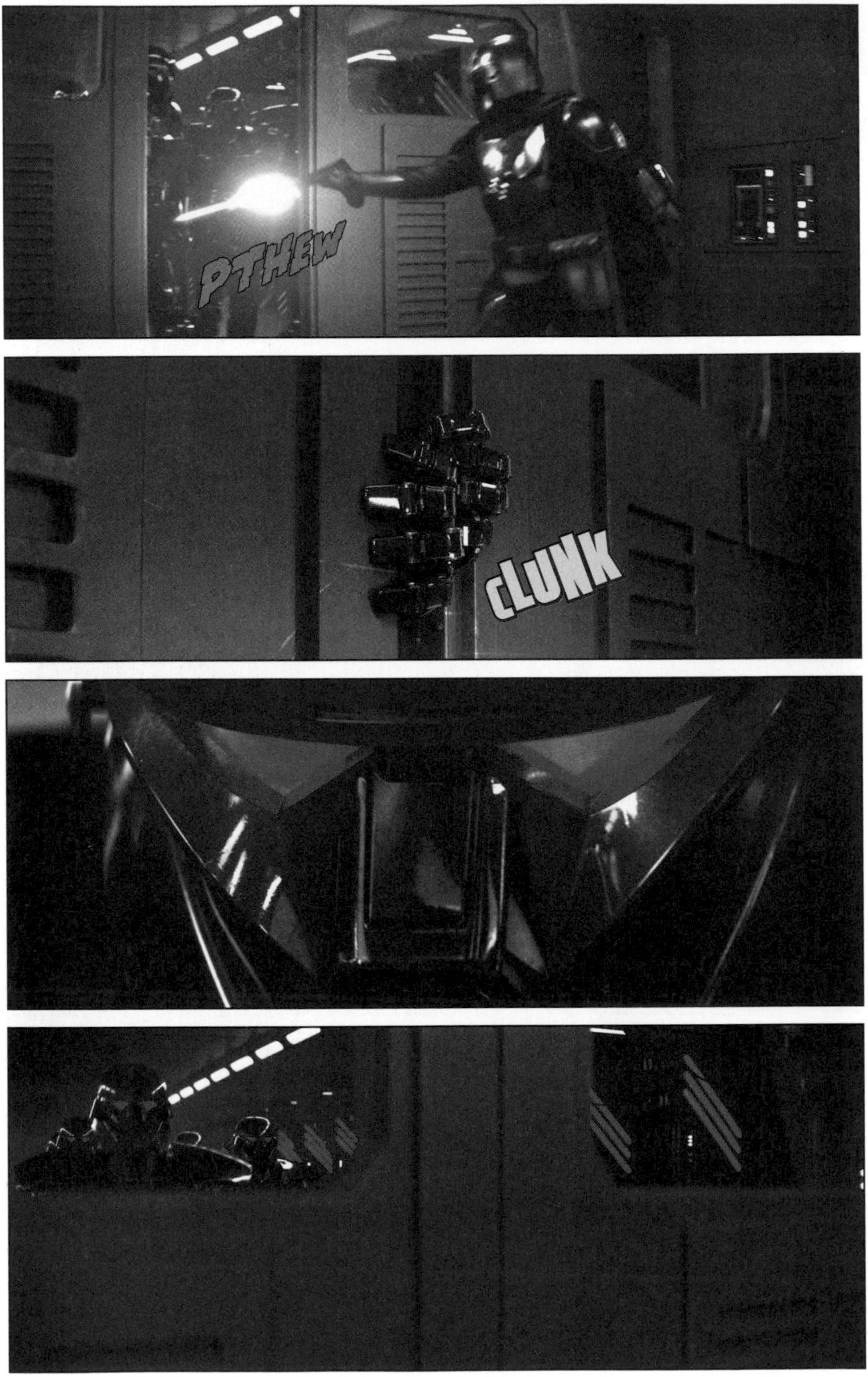
PTHEW
CLUNK

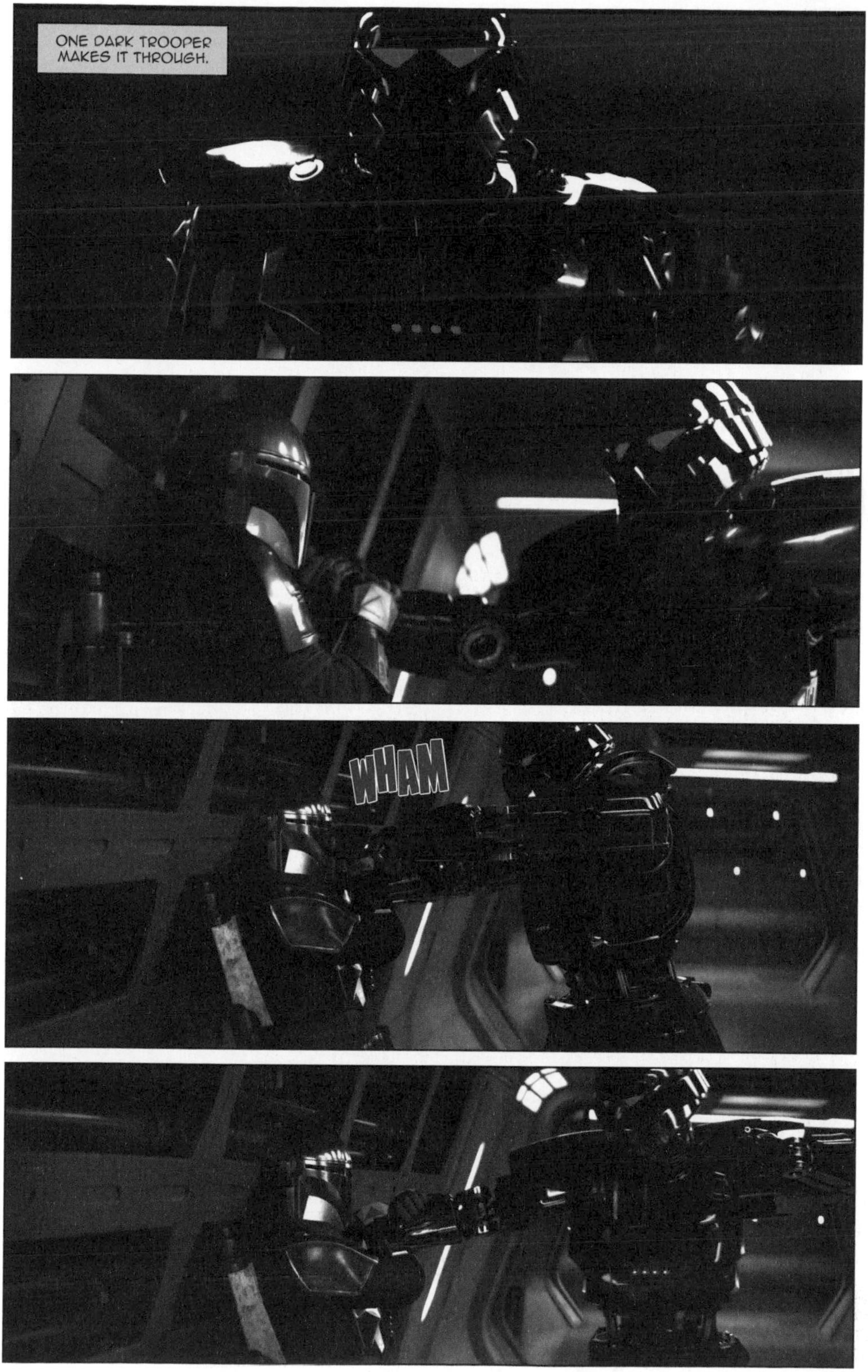
ONE DARK TROOPER
MAKES IT THROUGH.
WHAM

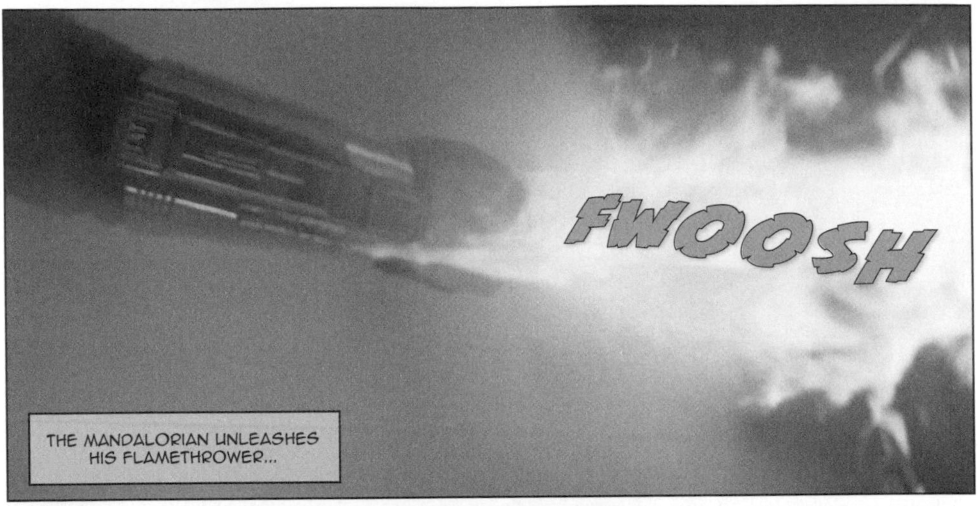
FWOOSH
THE MANDALORIAN UNLEASHES HIS FLAMETHROWER...

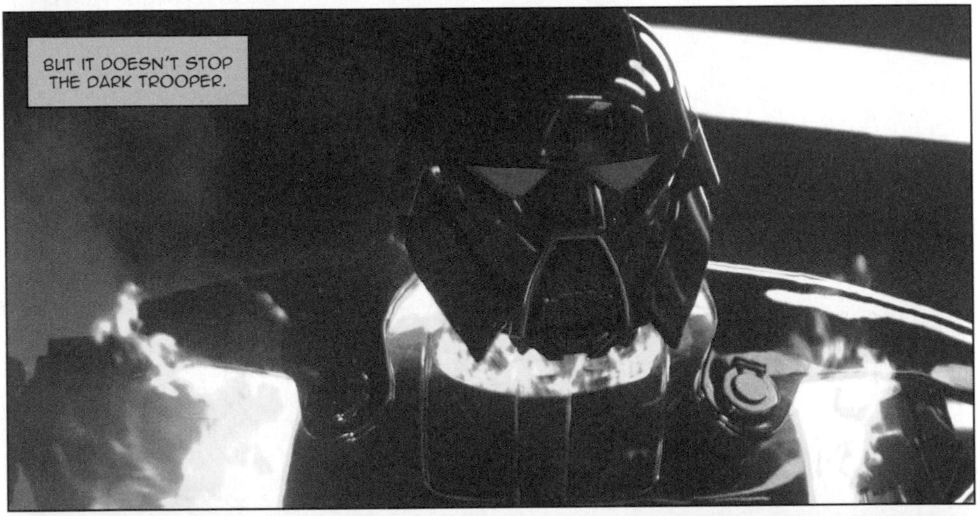
BUT IT DOESN'T STOP THE DARK TROOPER.

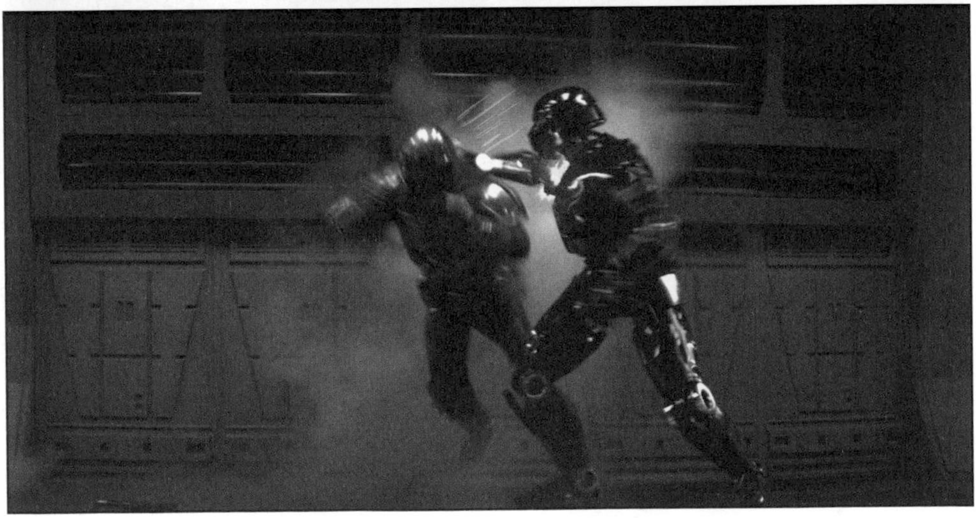

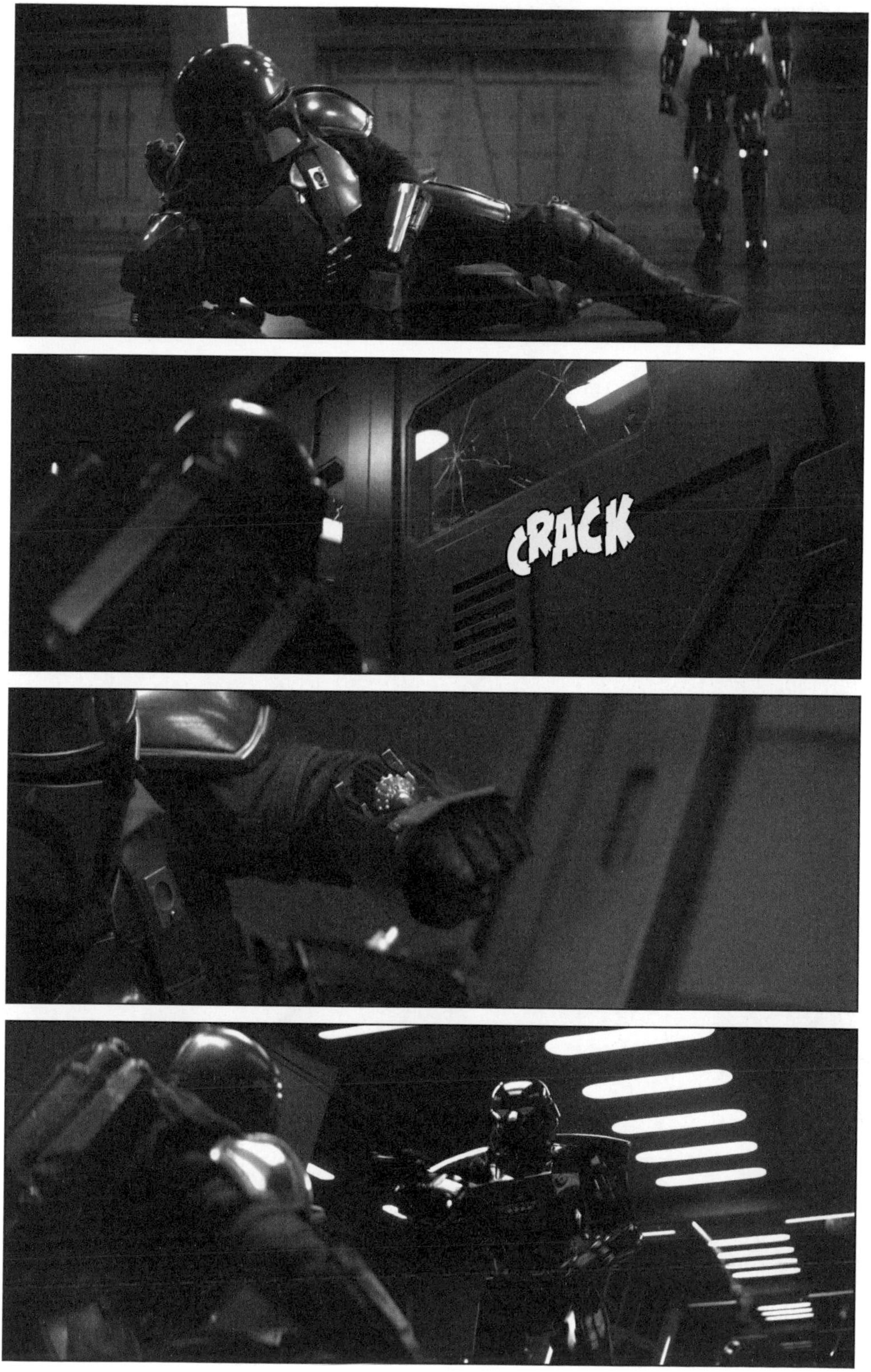
CRACK

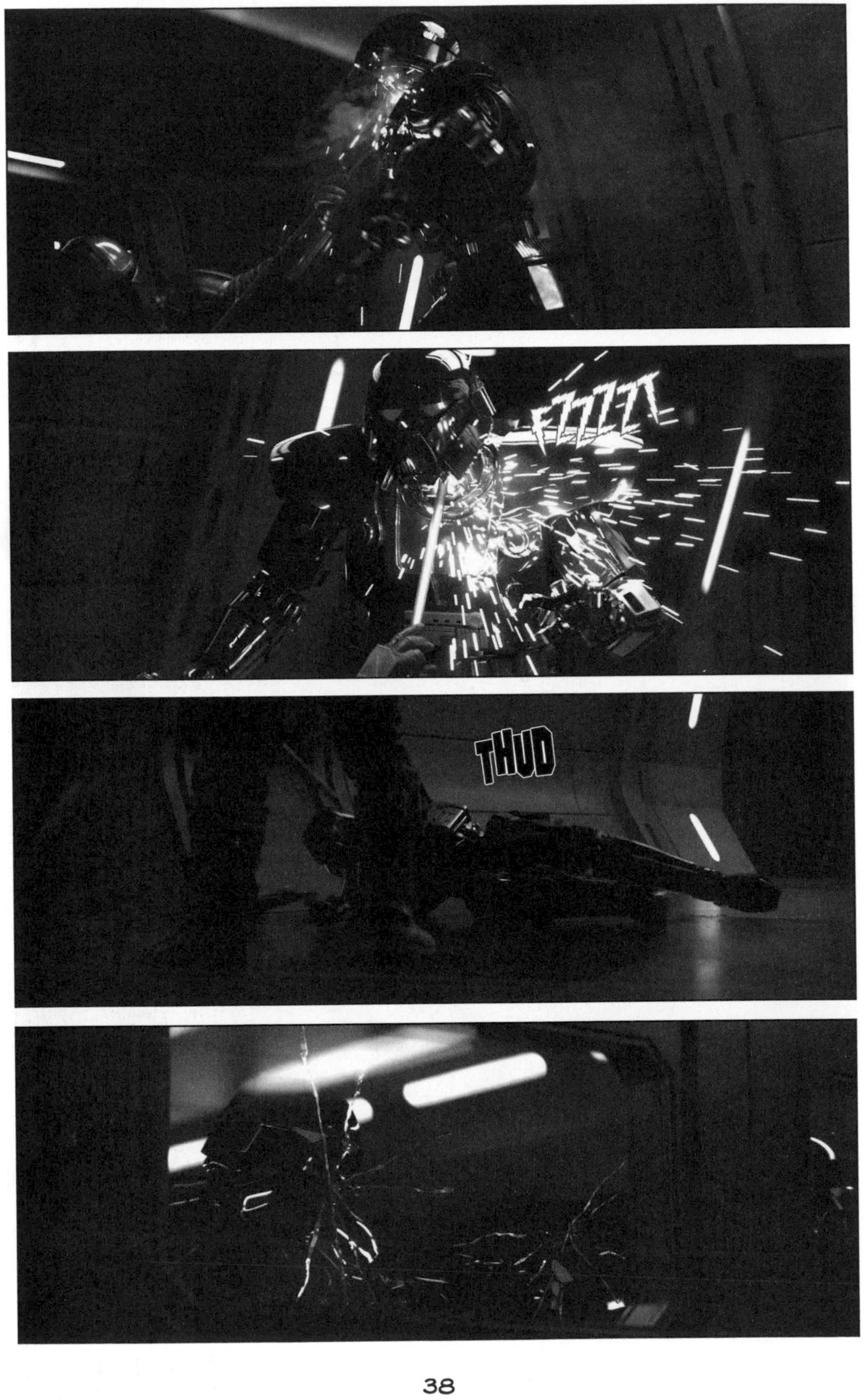
FZZZZT
THUD

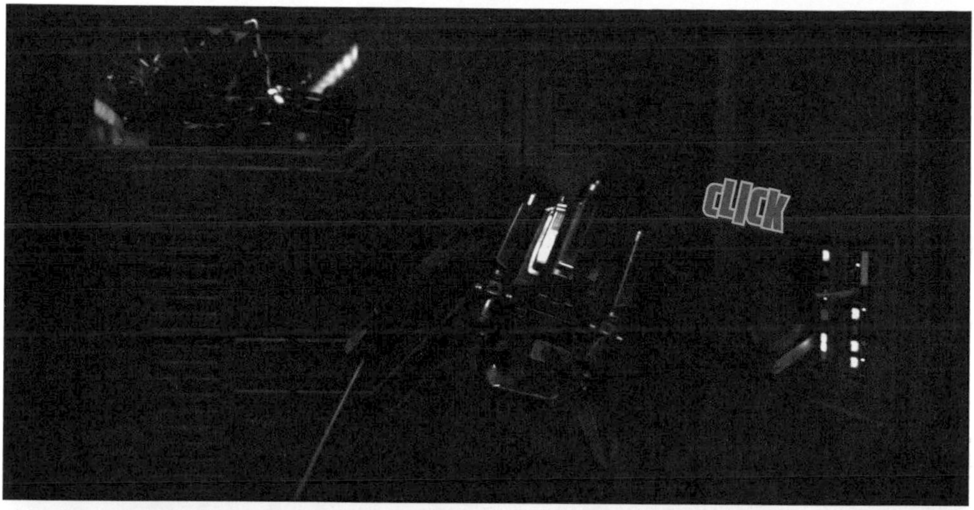
CLICK
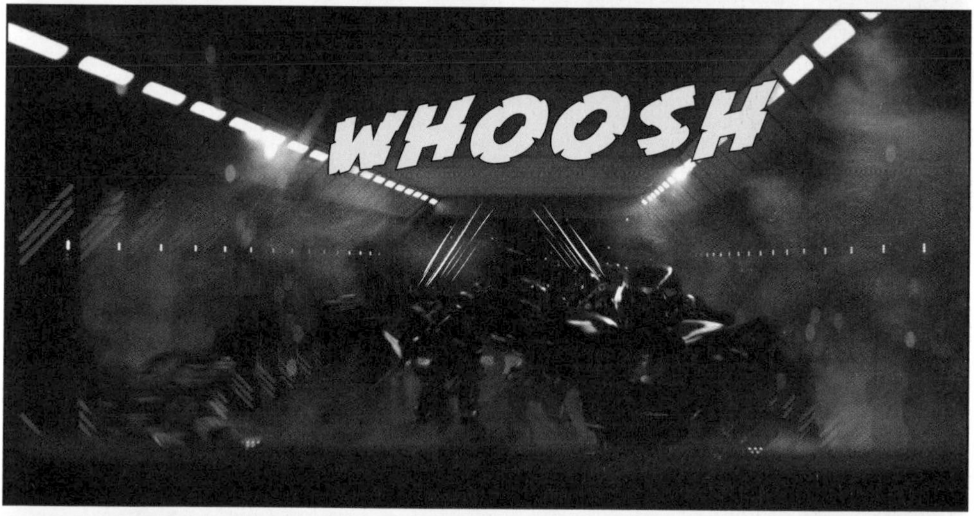
WHOOSH
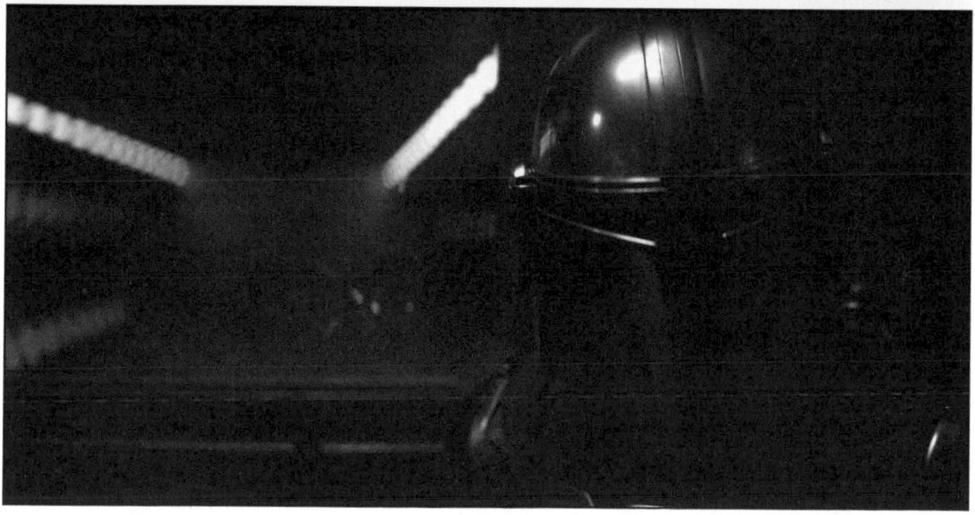

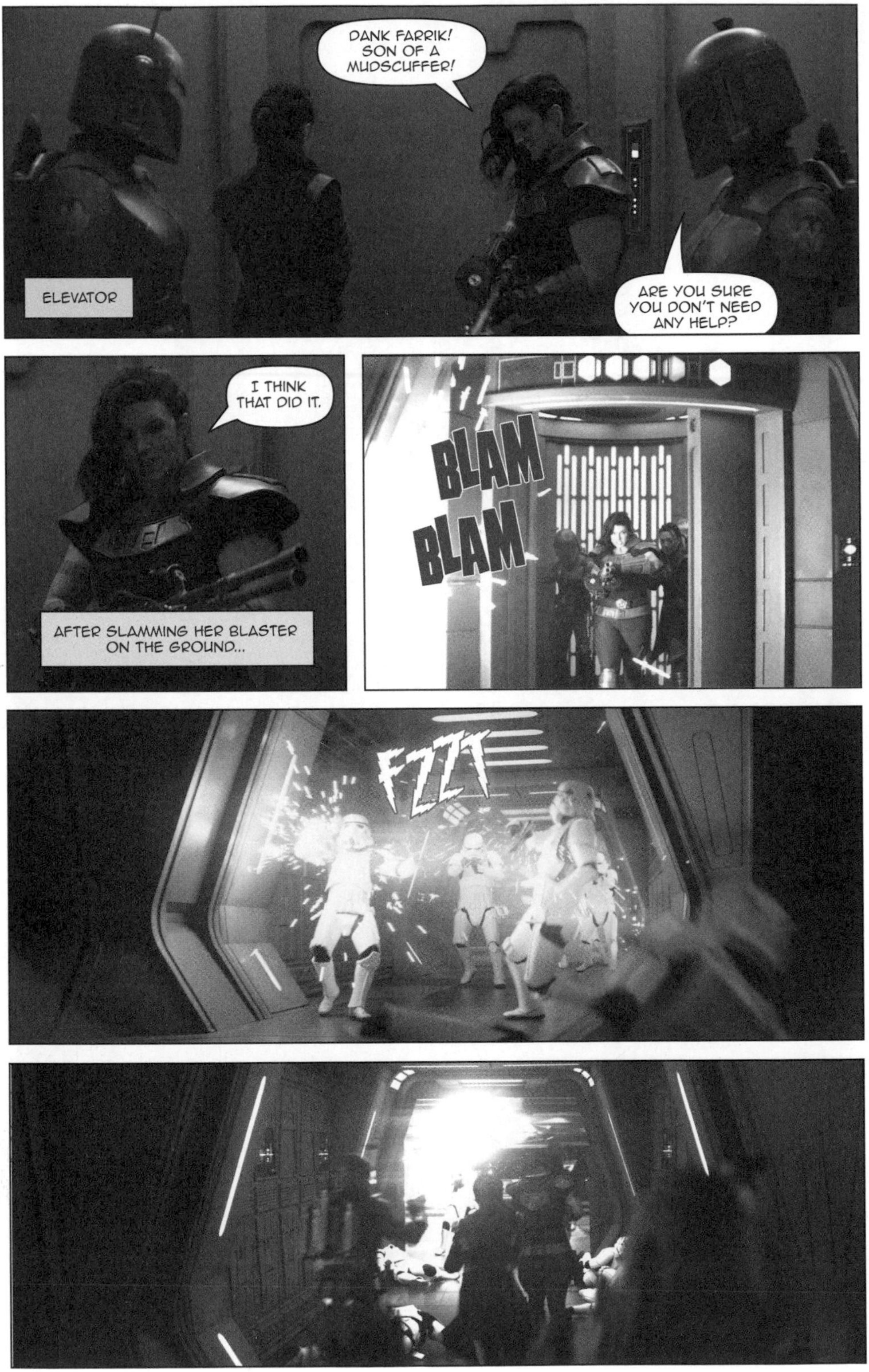
ELEVATOR
DANK FARRIK! SON OF A MUDSCUFFER!
ARE YOU SURE YOU DON'T NEED ANY HELP?
AFTER SLAMMING HER BLASTER ON THE GROUND...
I THINK THAT DID IT.
BLAM
BLAM
FZZT

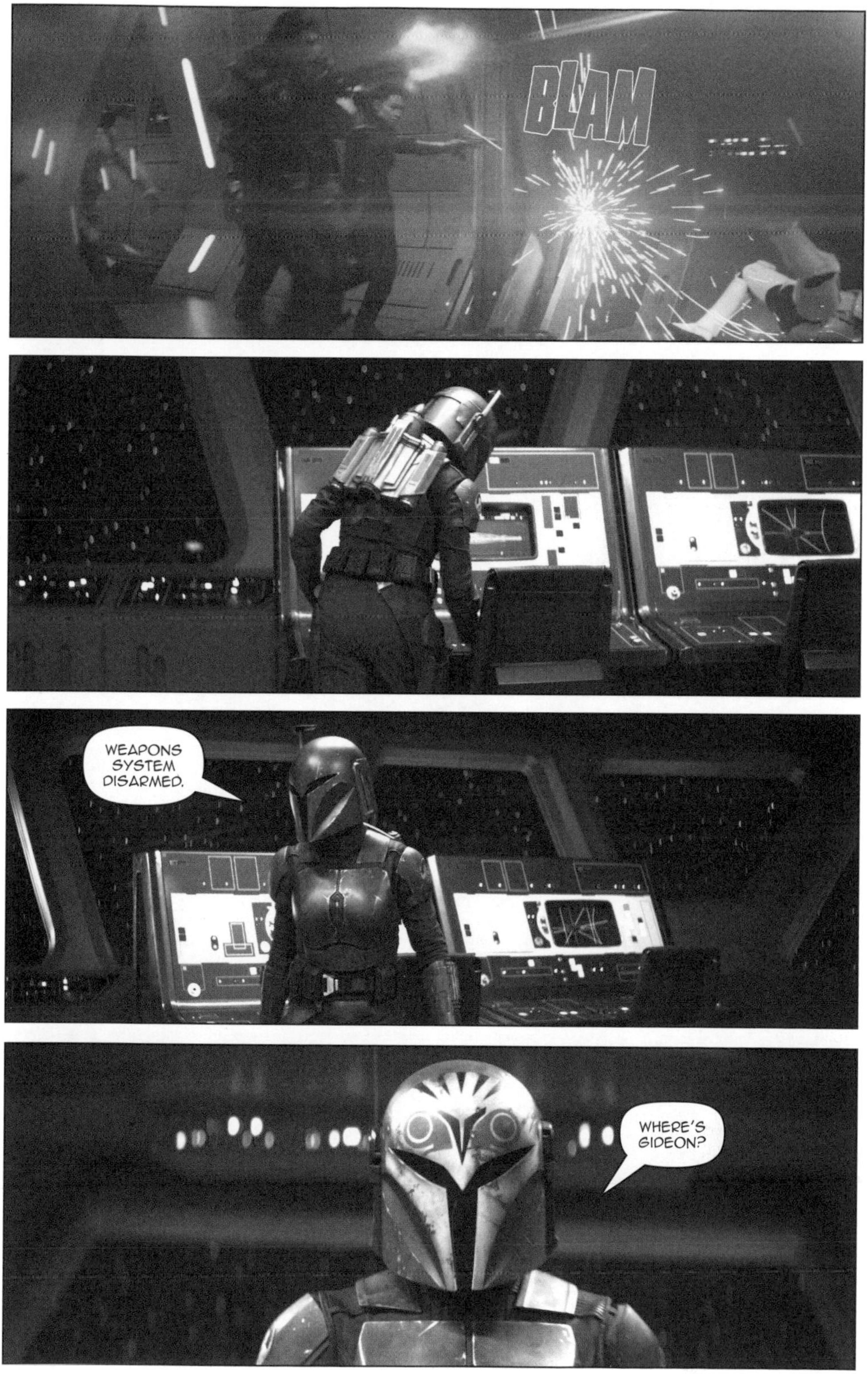
BLAM
WEAPONS SYSTEM DISARMED.
WHERE'S GIDEON?

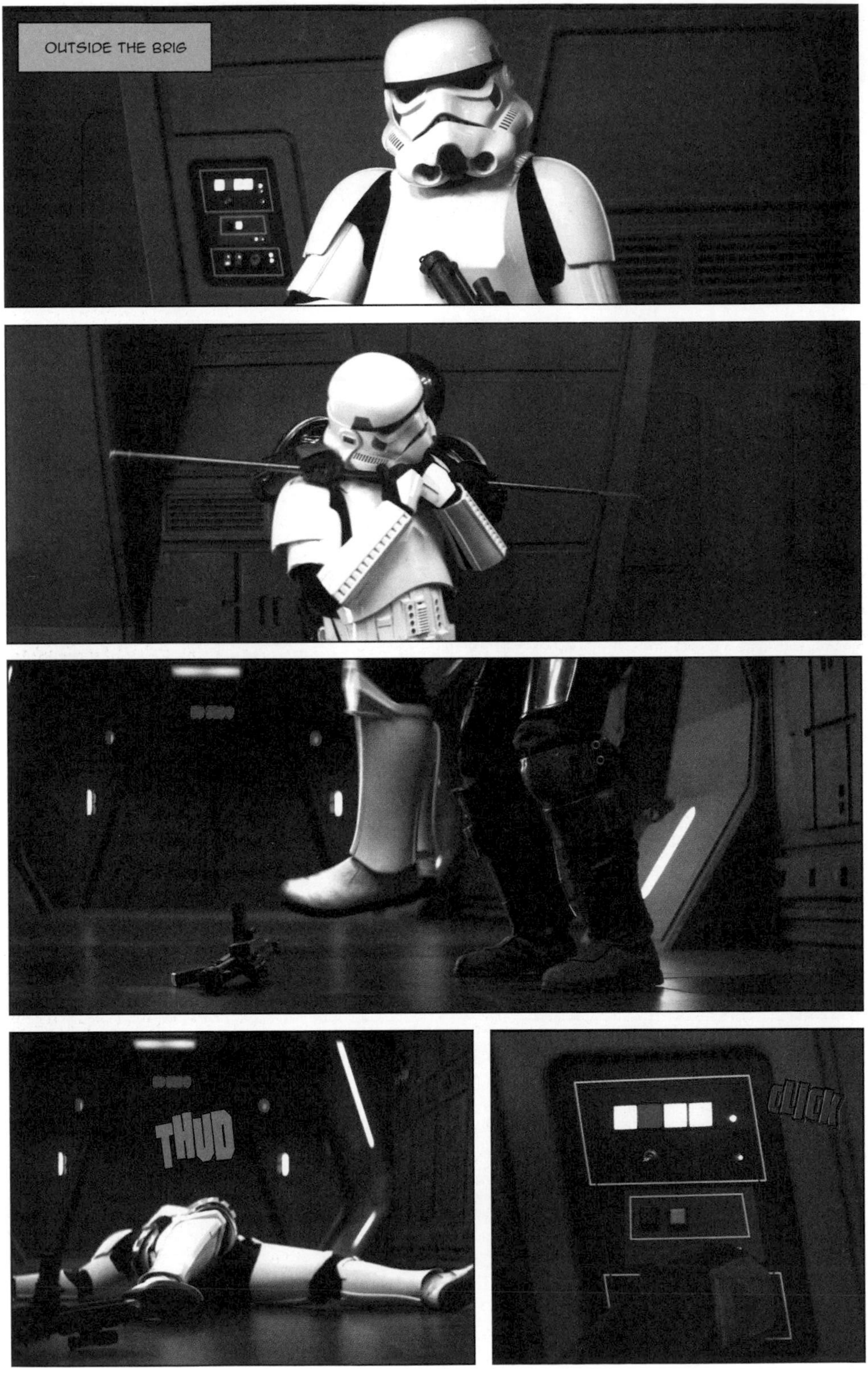
OUTSIDE THE BRIG
THUD
CLICK

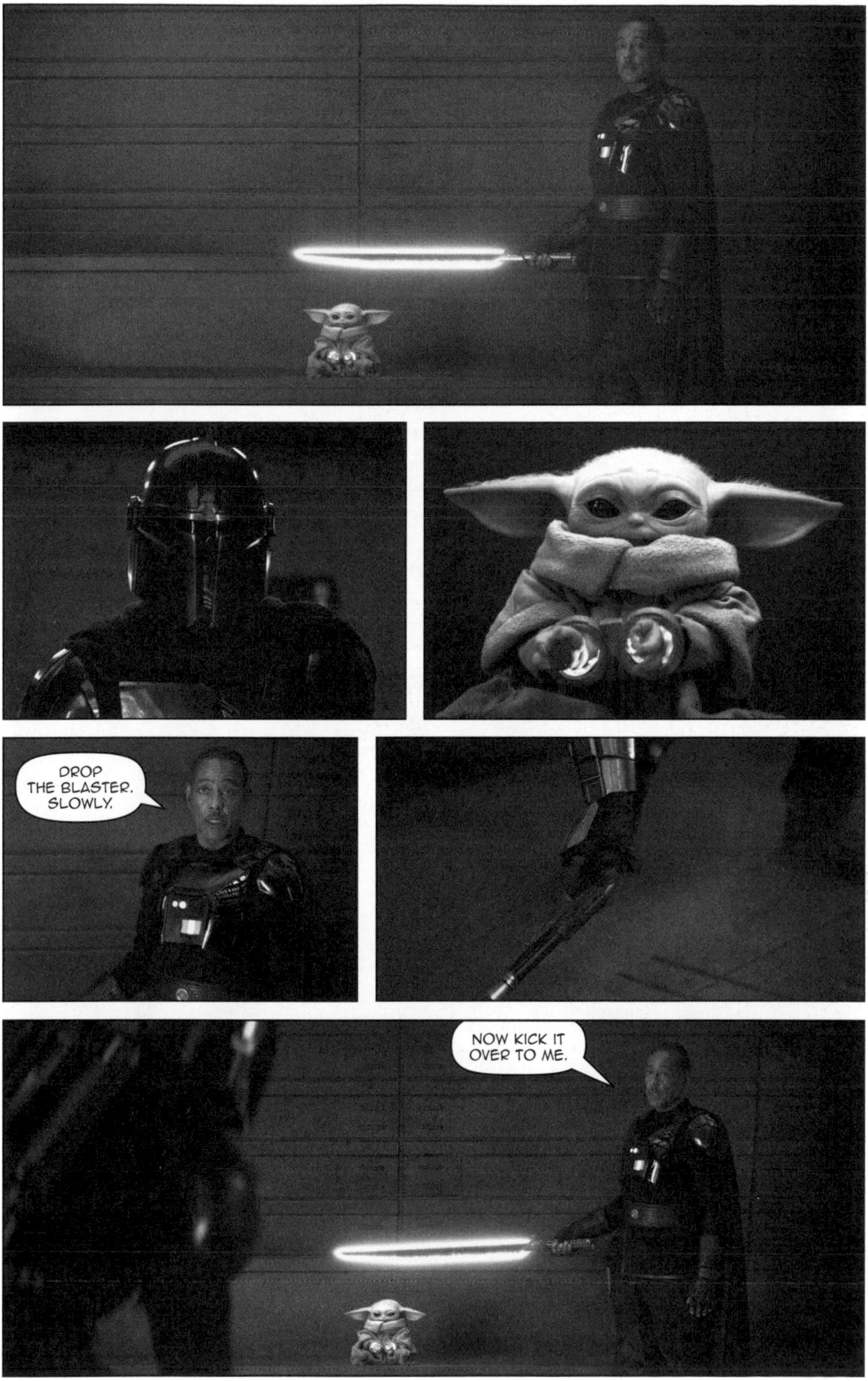
DROP THE BLASTER. SLOWLY.
NOW KICK IT OVER TO ME.

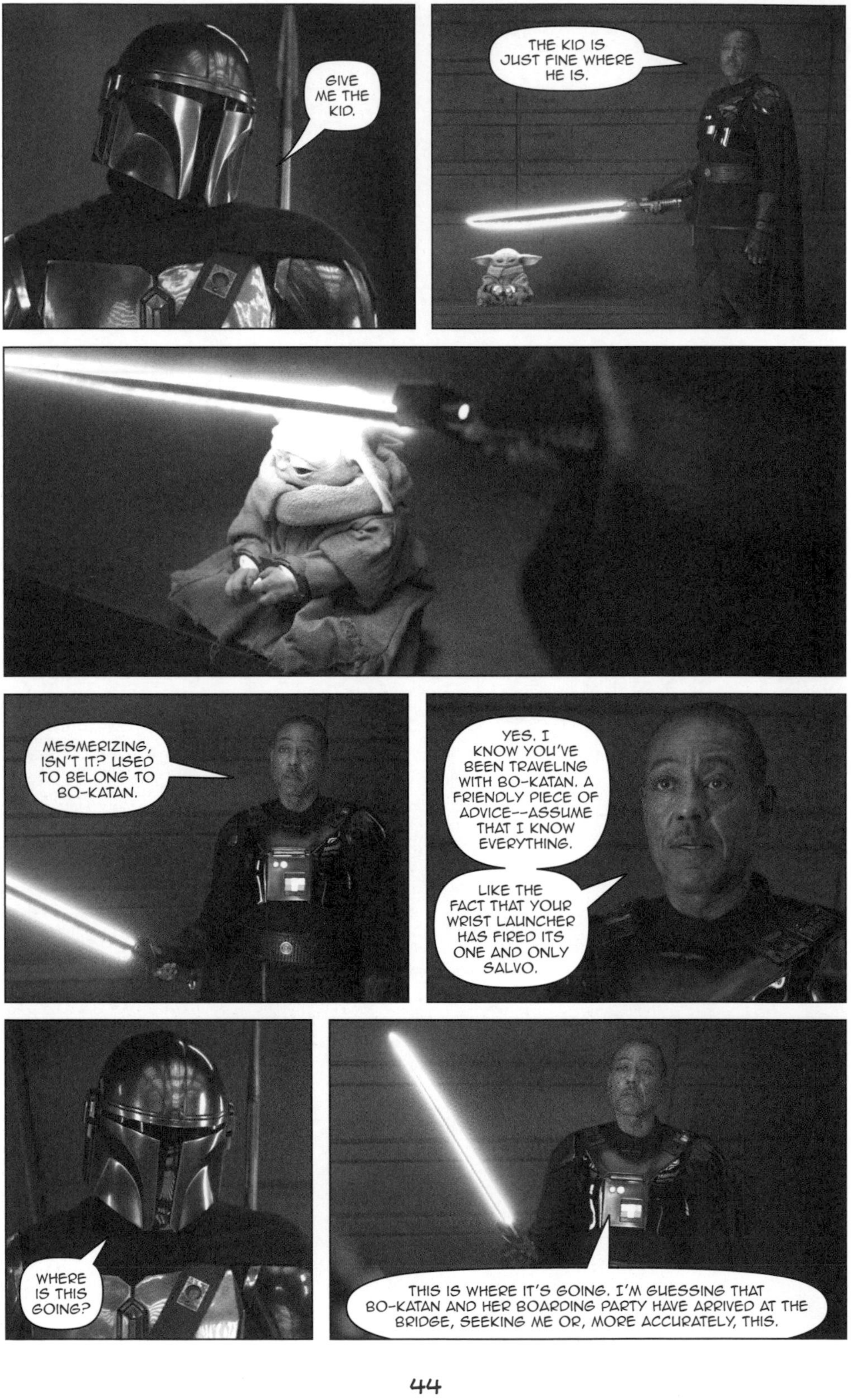
GIVE ME THE KID.
THE KID IS JUST FINE WHERE HE IS.
MESMERIZING, ISN'T IT? USED TO BELONG TO BO-KATAN.
YES. I KNOW YOU'VE BEEN TRAVELING WITH BO-KATAN. A FRIENDLY PIECE OF ADVICE--ASSUME THAT I KNOW EVERYTHING.
LIKE THE FACT THAT YOUR WRIST LAUNCHER HAS FIRED ITS ONE AND ONLY SALVO.
WHERE IS THIS GOING?
THIS IS WHERE IT'S GOING. I'M GUESSING THAT BO-KATAN AND HER BOARDING PARTY HAVE ARRIVED AT THE BRIDGE, SEEKING ME OR, MORE ACCURATELY, THIS.

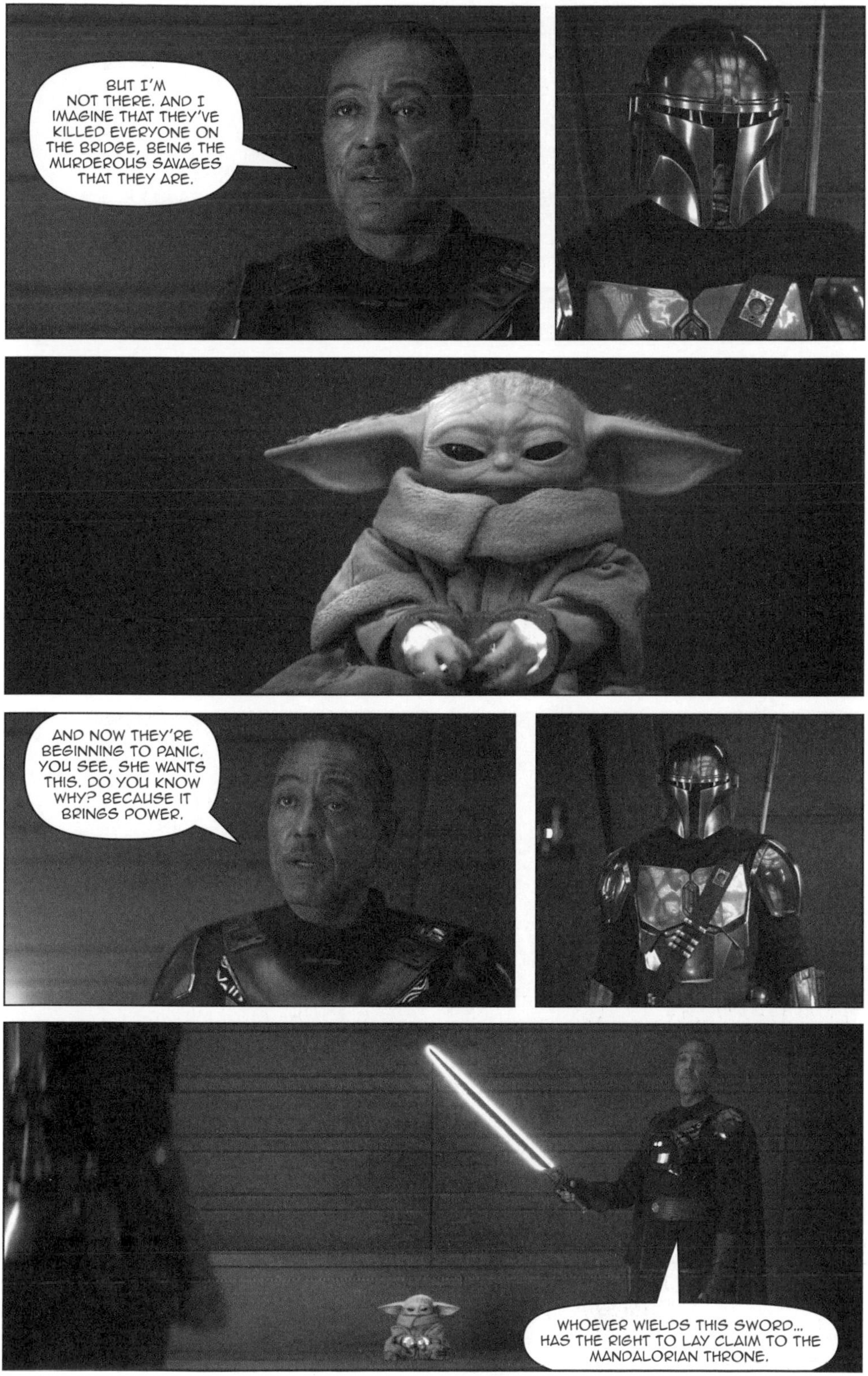
BUT I'M NOT THERE. AND I IMAGINE THAT THEY'VE KILLED EVERYONE ON THE BRIDGE, BEING THE MURDEROUS SAVAGES THAT THEY ARE.
AND NOW THEY'RE BEGINNING TO PANIC. YOU SEE, SHE WANTS THIS. DO YOU KNOW WHY? BECAUSE IT BRINGS POWER.
WHOEVER WIELDS THIS SWORD... HAS THE RIGHT TO LAY CLAIM TO THE MANDALORIAN THRONE.

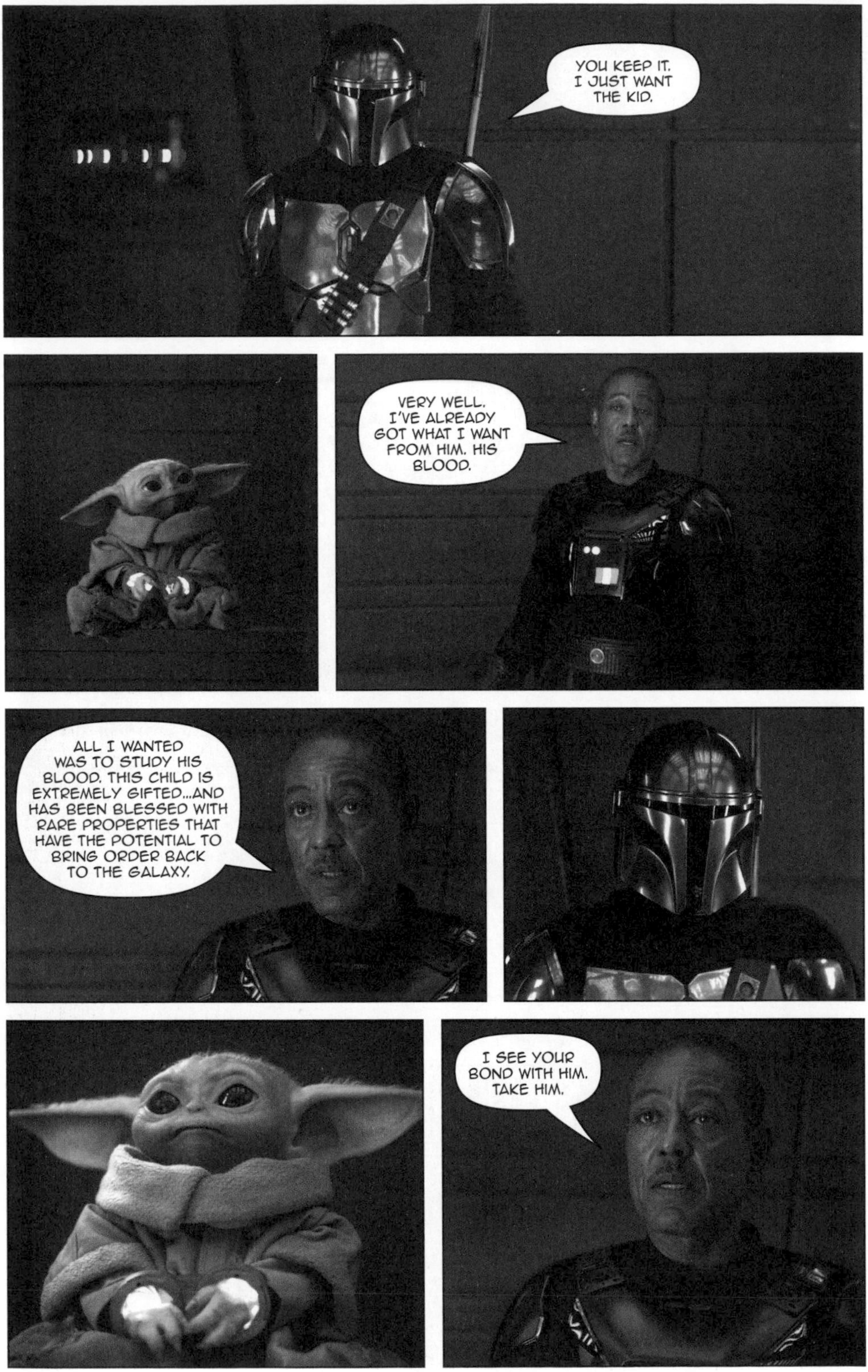
YOU KEEP IT. I JUST WANT THE KID.
VERY WELL. I'VE ALREADY GOT WHAT I WANT FROM HIM. HIS BLOOD.
ALL I WANTED WAS TO STUDY HIS BLOOD. THIS CHILD IS EXTREMELY GIFTED...AND HAS BEEN BLESSED WITH RARE PROPERTIES THAT HAVE THE POTENTIAL TO BRING ORDER BACK TO THE GALAXY.
I SEE YOUR BOND WITH HIM. TAKE HIM.

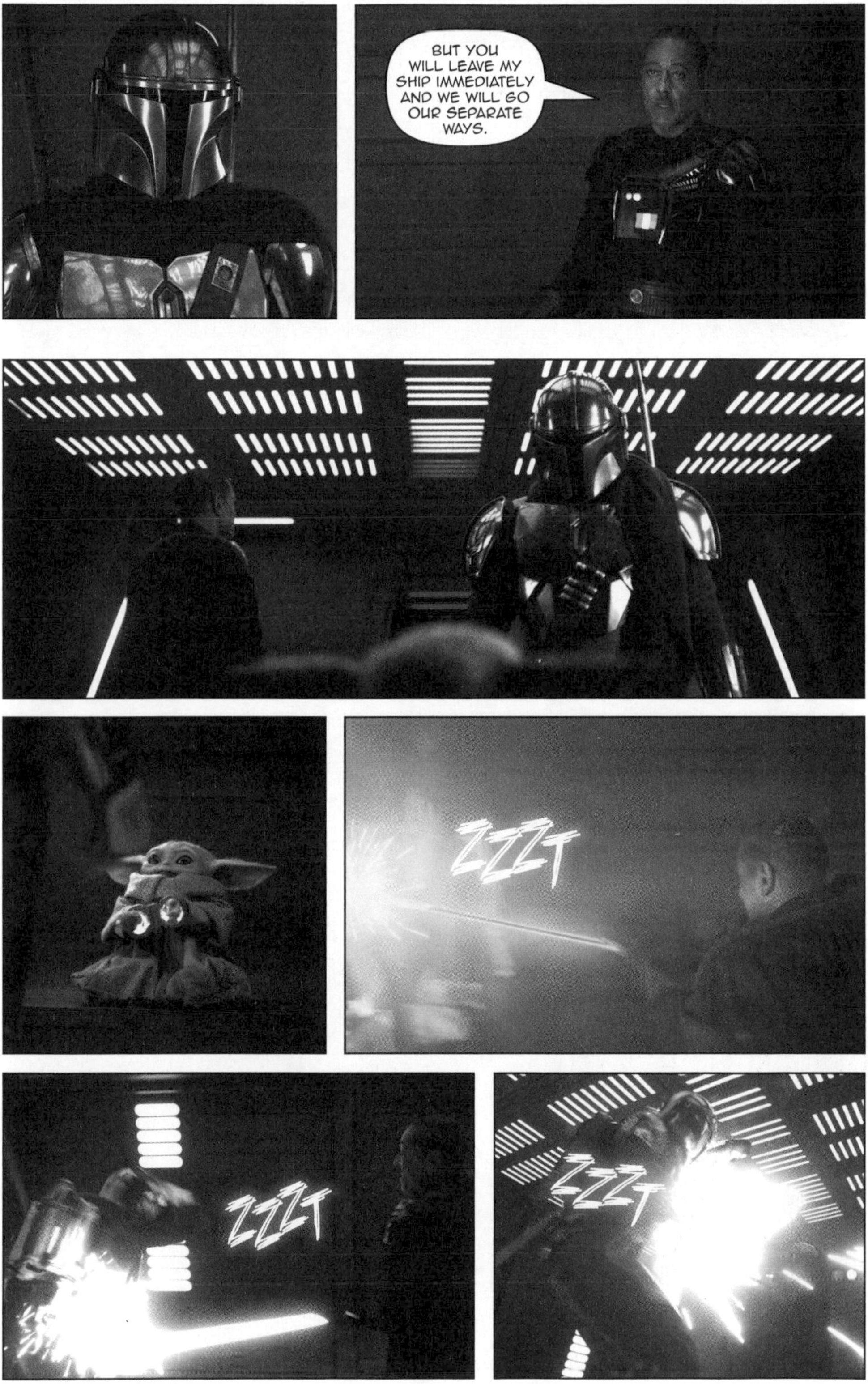
BUT YOU WILL LEAVE MY SHIP IMMEDIATELY AND WE WILL GO OUR SEPARATE WAYS.
ZZZT
ZZZT
ZZZT

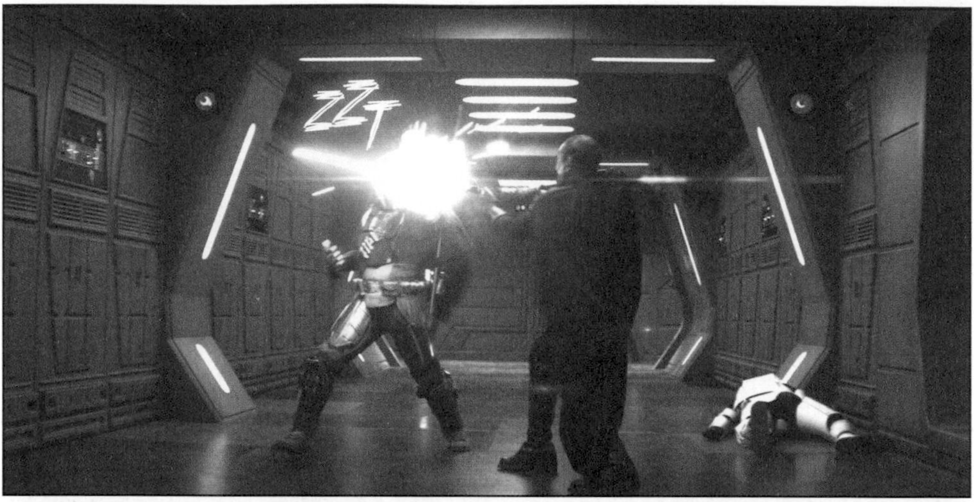
ZZT

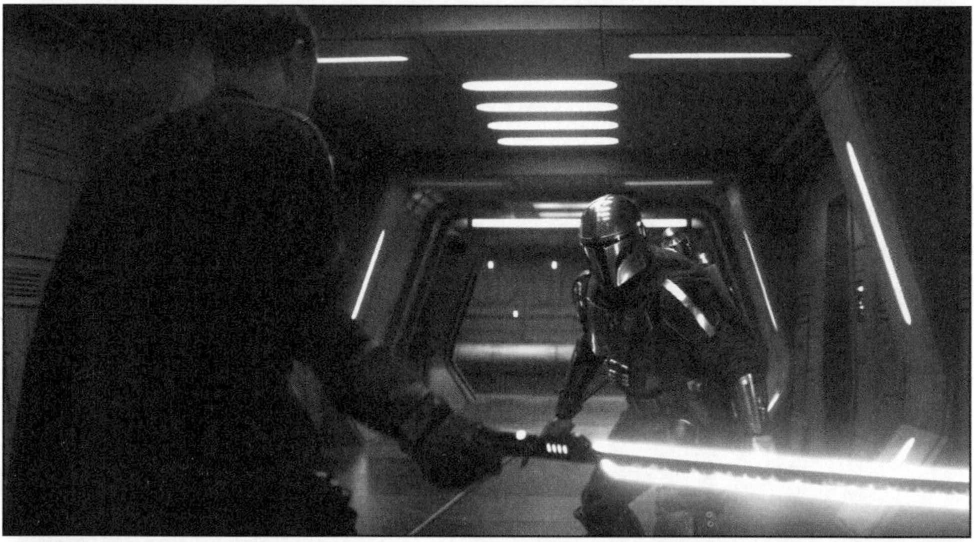

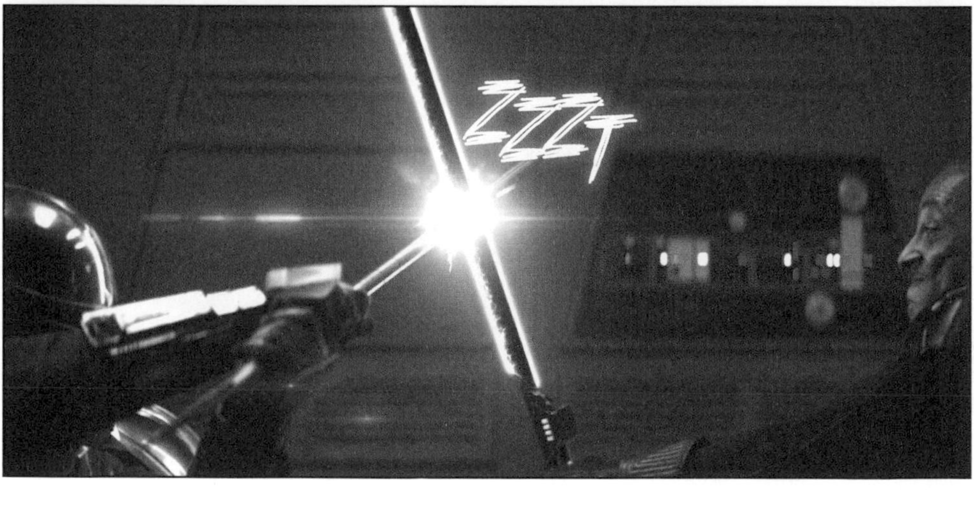
ZZZT

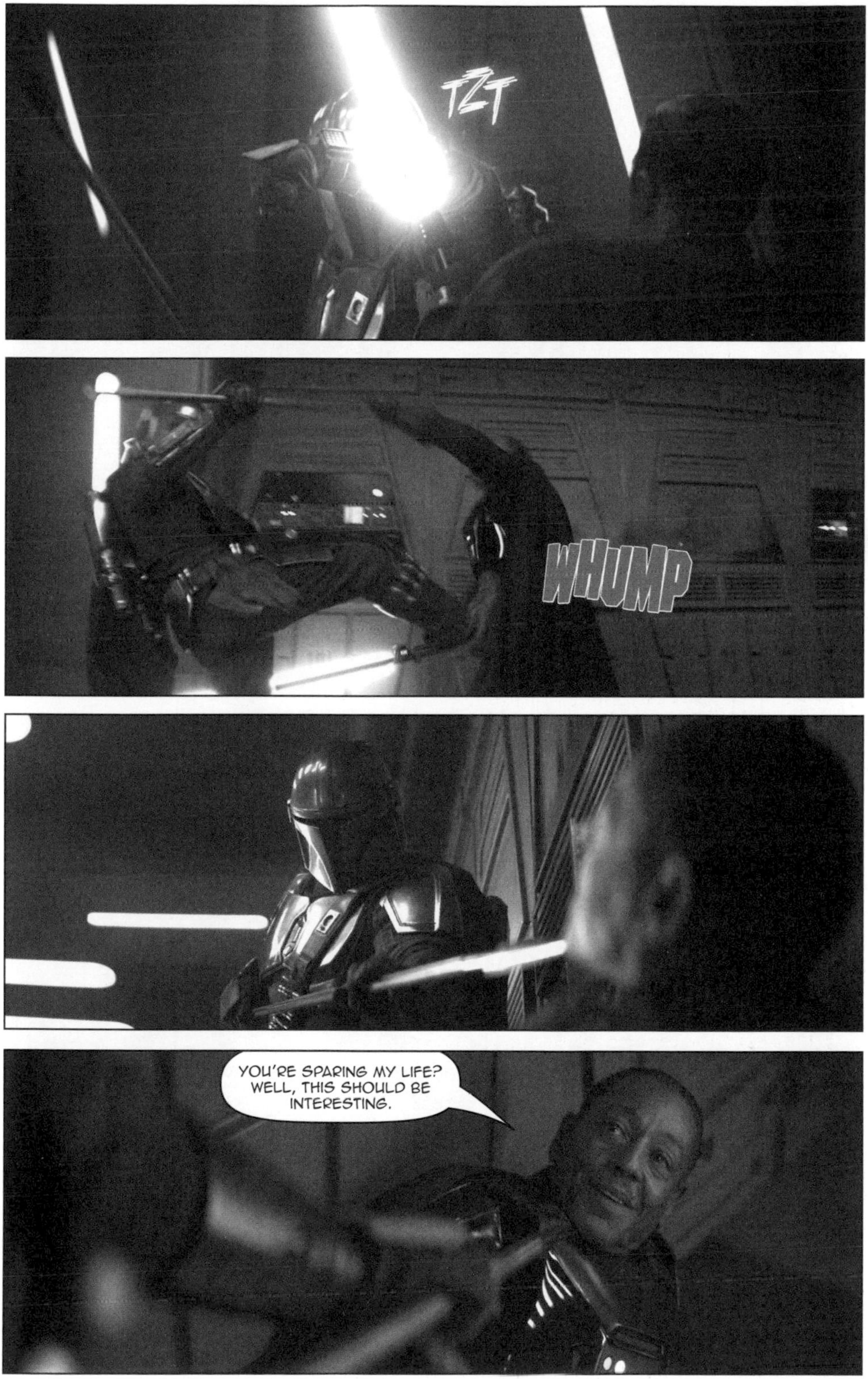
TZT
WHUMP
YOU'RE SPARING MY LIFE? WELL, THIS SHOULD BE INTERESTING.

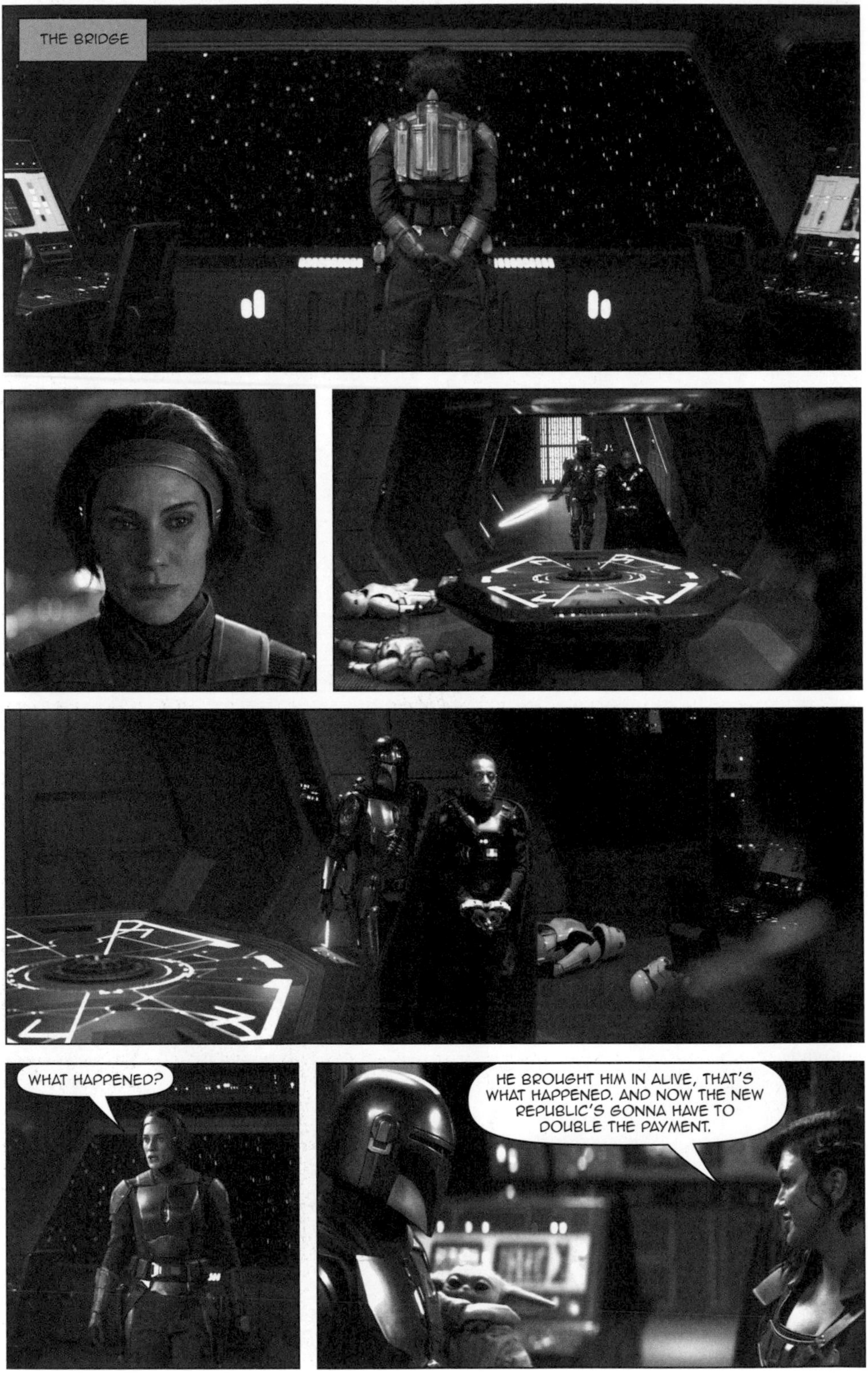
THE BRIDGE
WHAT HAPPENED?
HE BROUGHT HIM IN ALIVE, THAT'S WHAT HAPPENED. AND NOW THE NEW REPUBLIC'S GONNA HAVE TO DOUBLE THE PAYMENT.

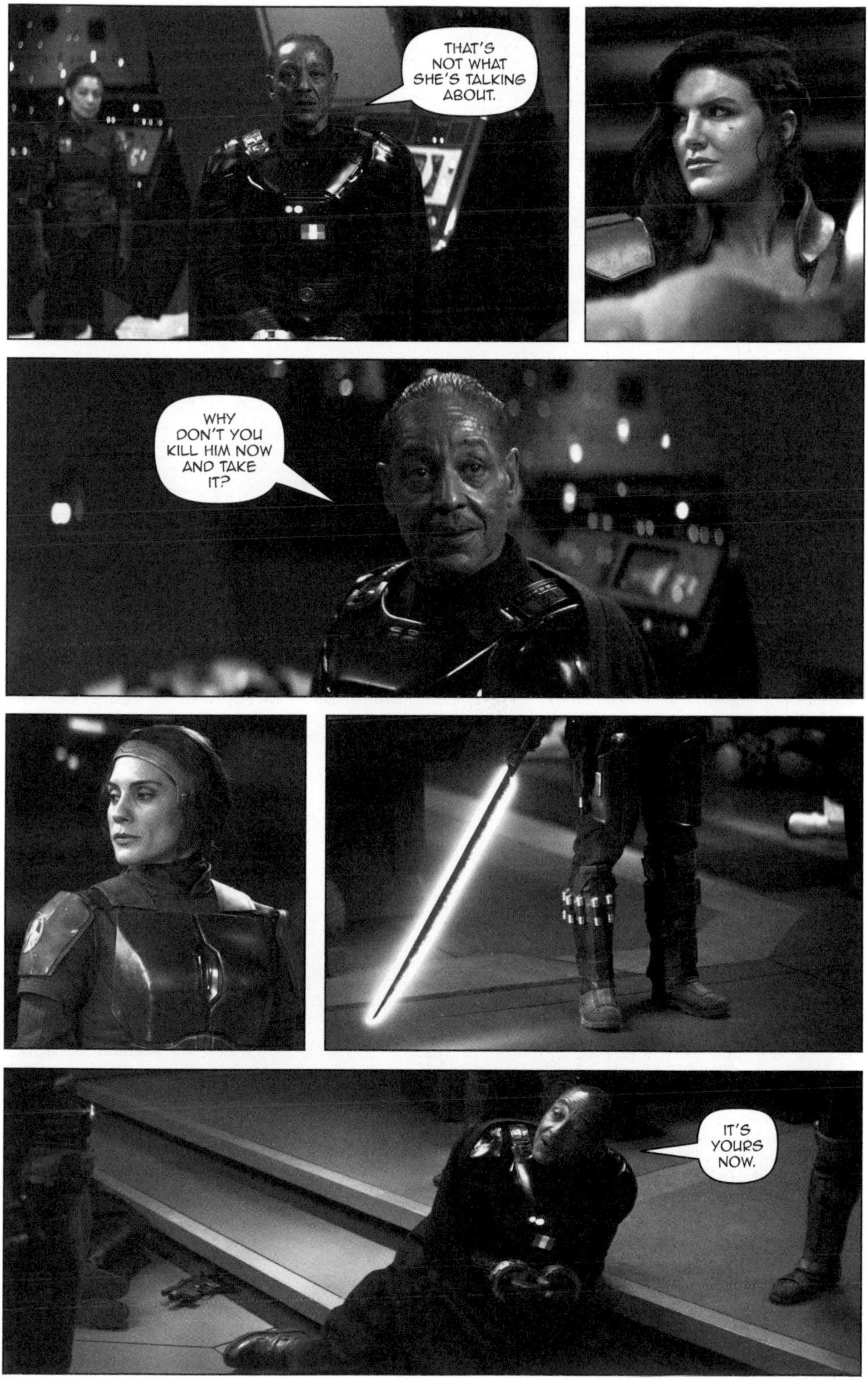
THAT'S NOT WHAT SHE'S TALKING ABOUT.
WHY DON'T YOU KILL HIM NOW AND TAKE IT?
IT'S YOURS NOW.

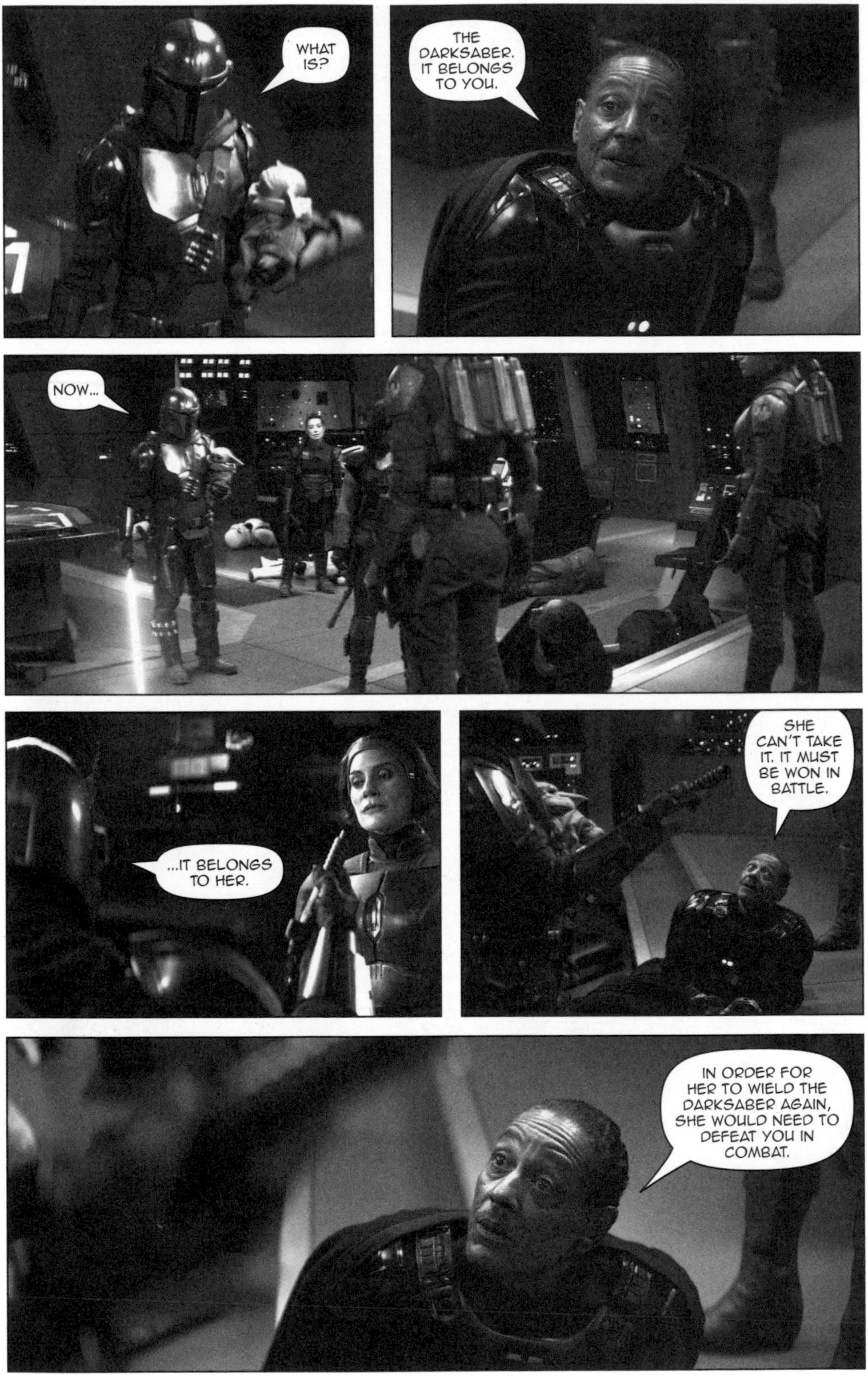
WHAT IS?
THE DARKSABER. IT BELONGS TO YOU.
NOW...
...IT BELONGS TO HER.
SHE CAN'T TAKE IT. IT MUST BE WON IN BATTLE.
IN ORDER FOR HER TO WIELD THE DARKSABER AGAIN, SHE WOULD NEED TO DEFEAT YOU IN COMBAT.

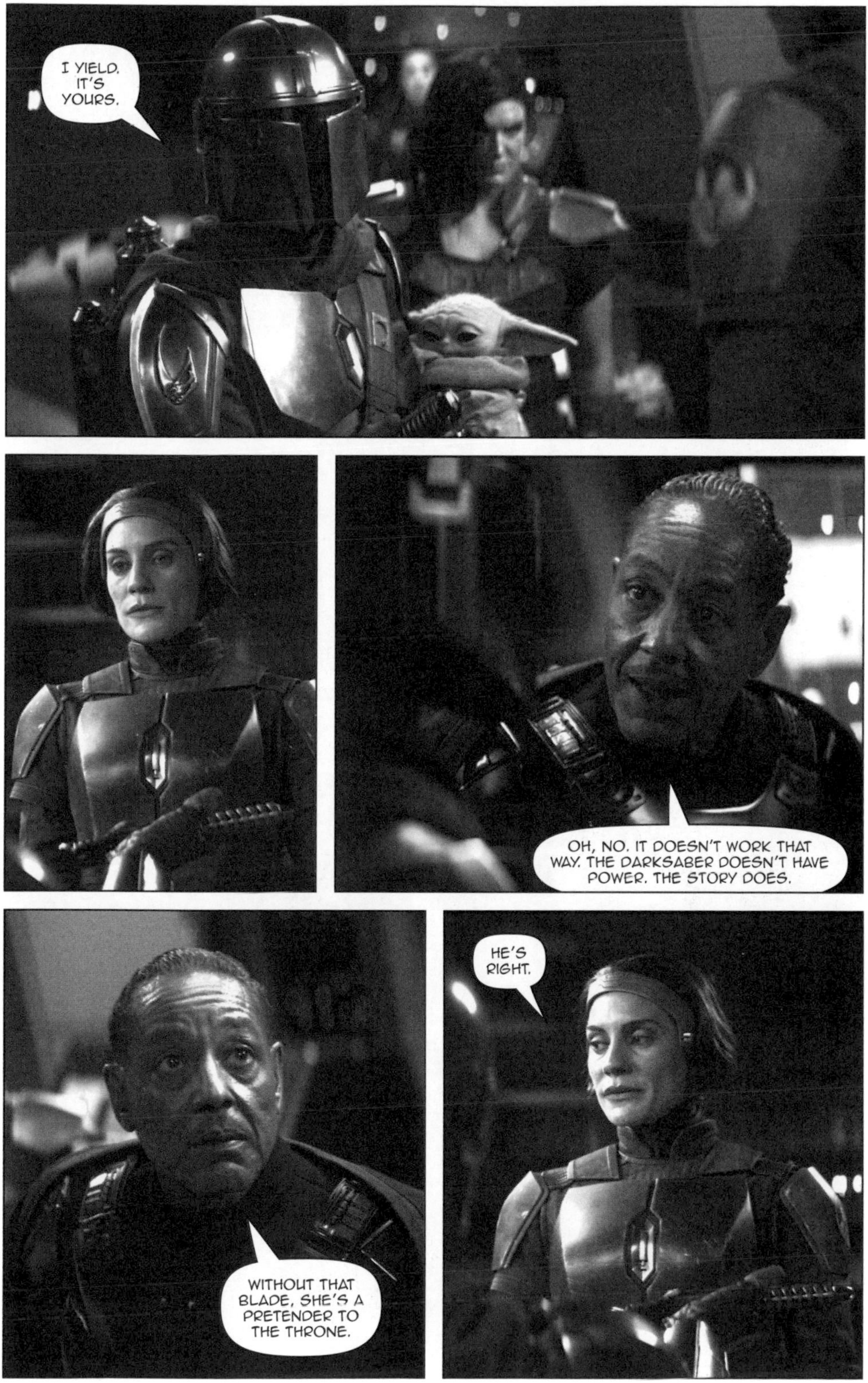
I YIELD. IT'S YOURS.
OH, NO. IT DOESN'T WORK THAT WAY. THE DARKSABER DOESN'T HAVE POWER. THE STORY DOES.
WITHOUT THAT BLADE, SHE'S A PRETENDER TO THE THRONE.
HE'S RIGHT.

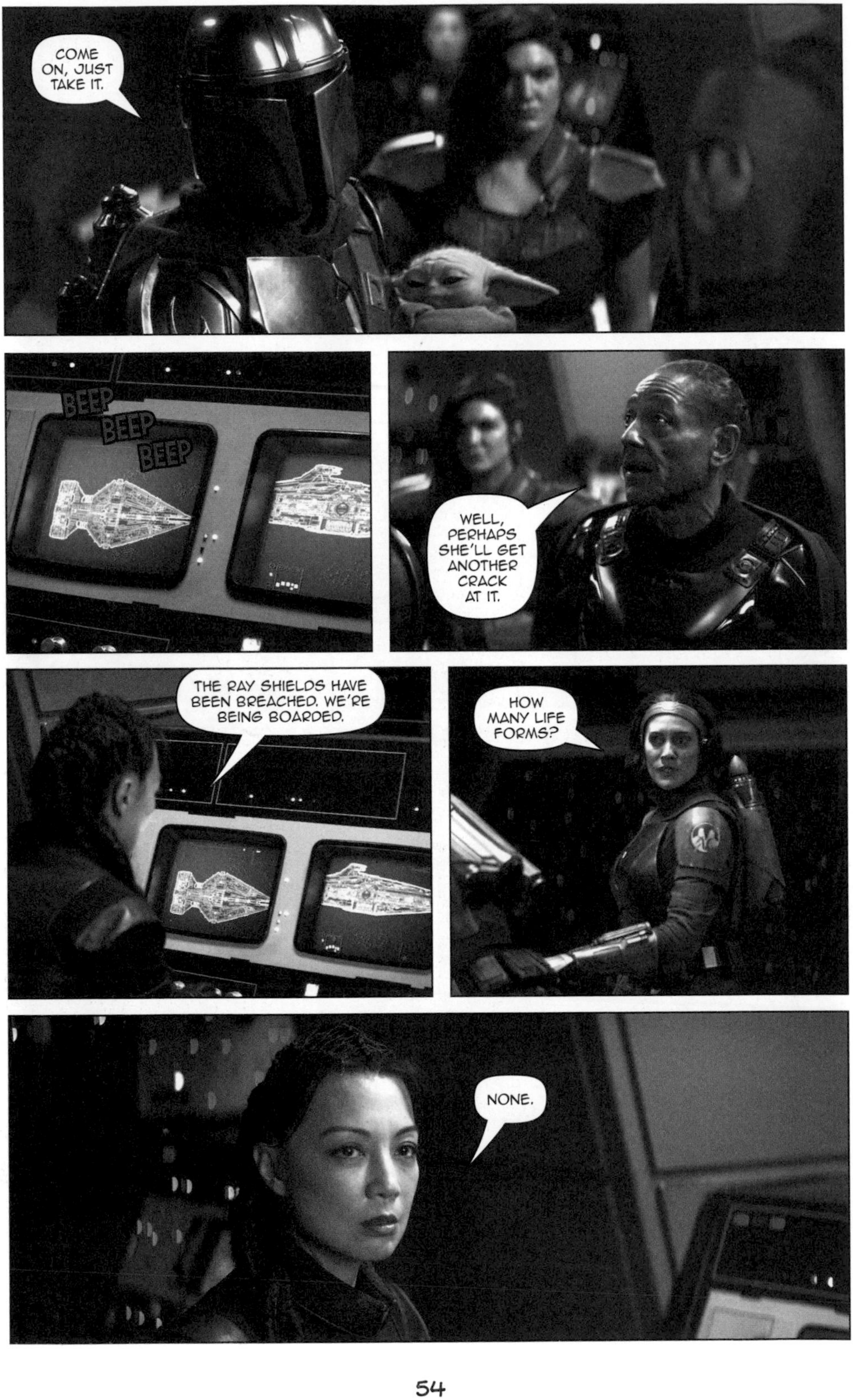
COME ON, JUST TAKE IT.
BEEP
BEEP
BEEP
WELL, PERHAPS SHE'LL GET ANOTHER CRACK AT IT.
THE RAY SHIELDS HAVE BEEN BREACHED. WE'RE BEING BOARDED.
HOW MANY LIFE FORMS?
NONE.

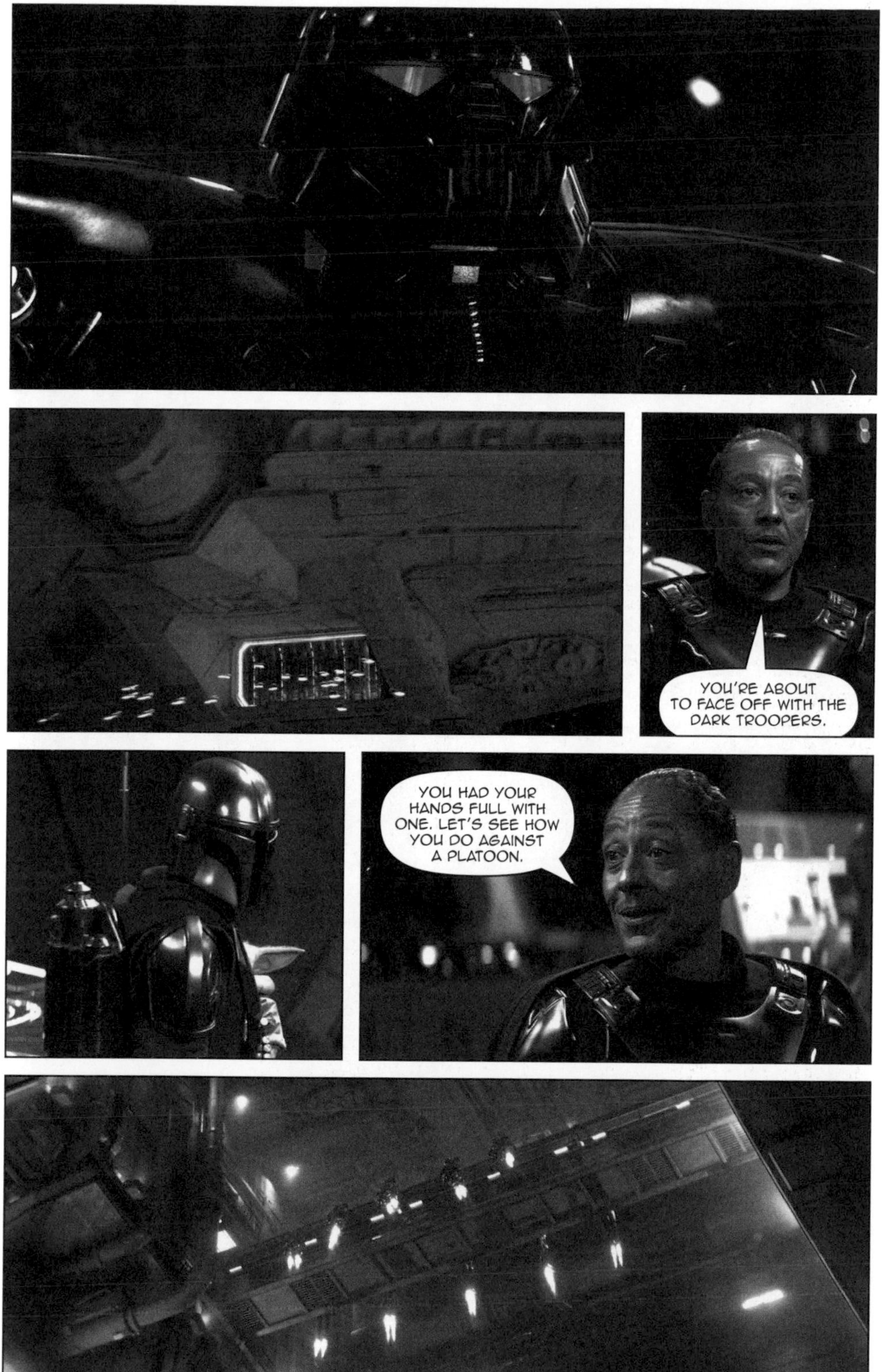
YOU'RE ABOUT TO FACE OFF WITH THE DARK TROOPERS.
YOU HAD YOUR HANDS FULL WITH ONE. LET'S SEE HOW YOU DO AGAINST A PLATOON.

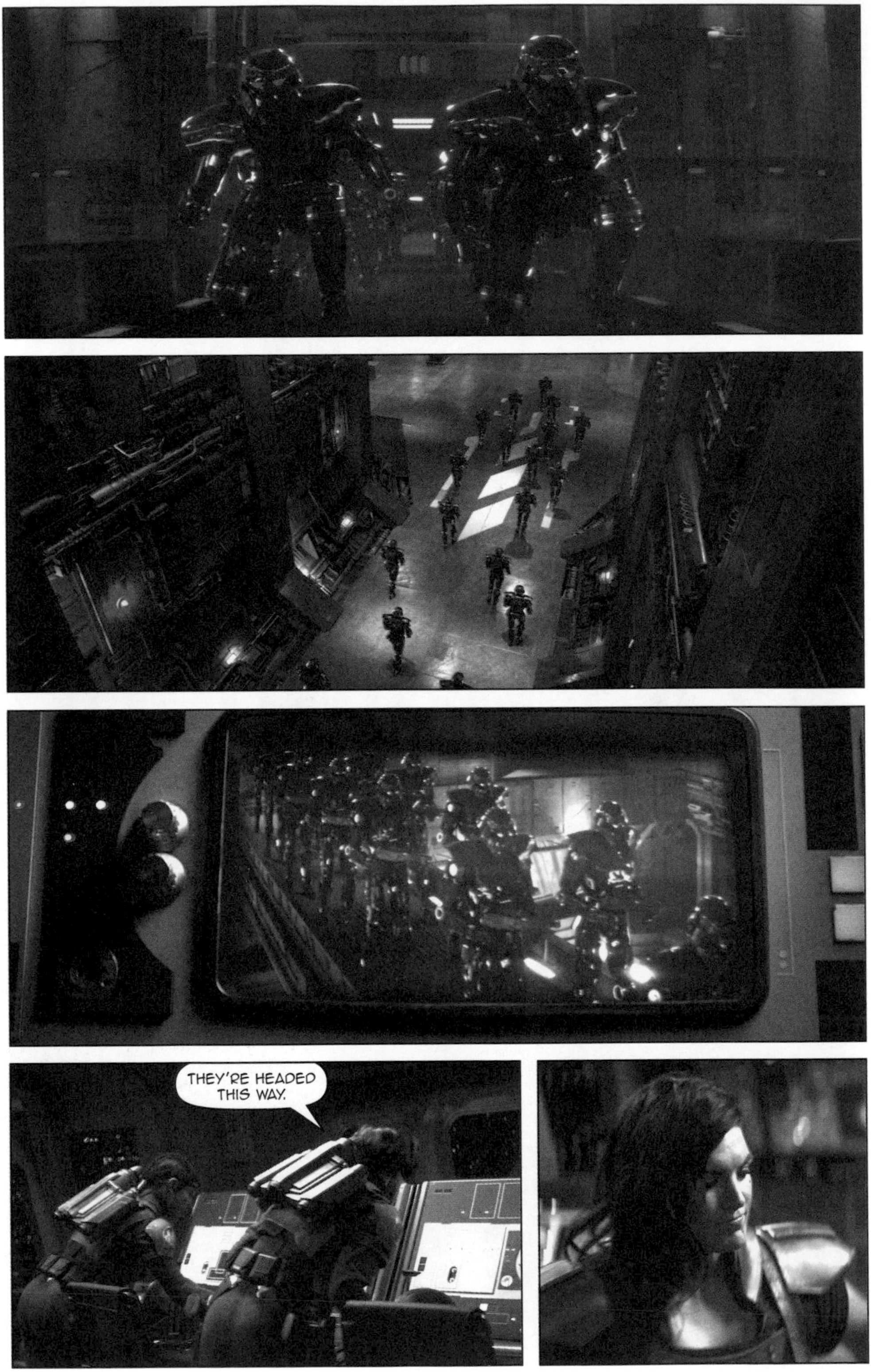
THEY'RE HEADED THIS WAY.

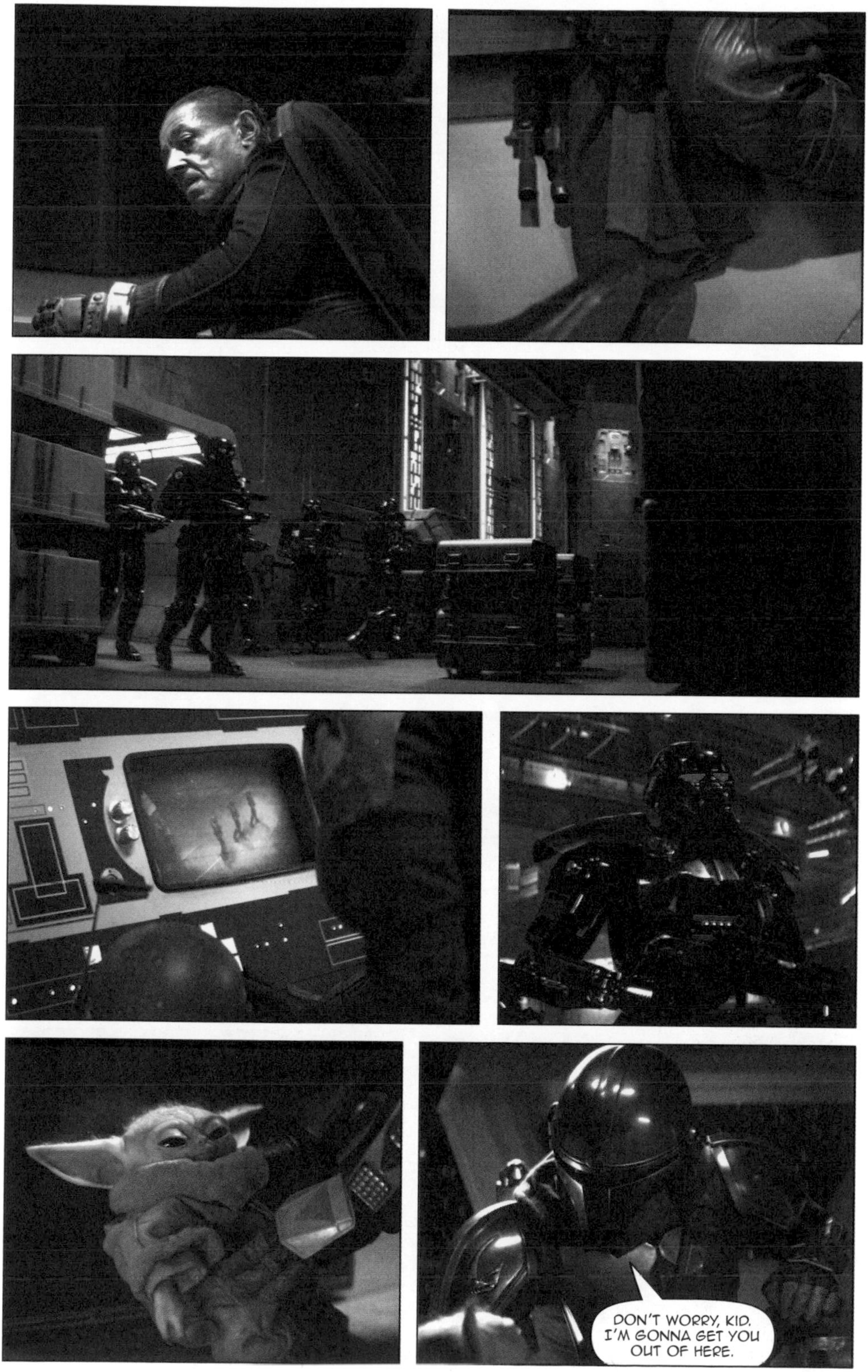
DON'T WORRY, KID. I'M GONNA GET YOU OUT OF HERE.

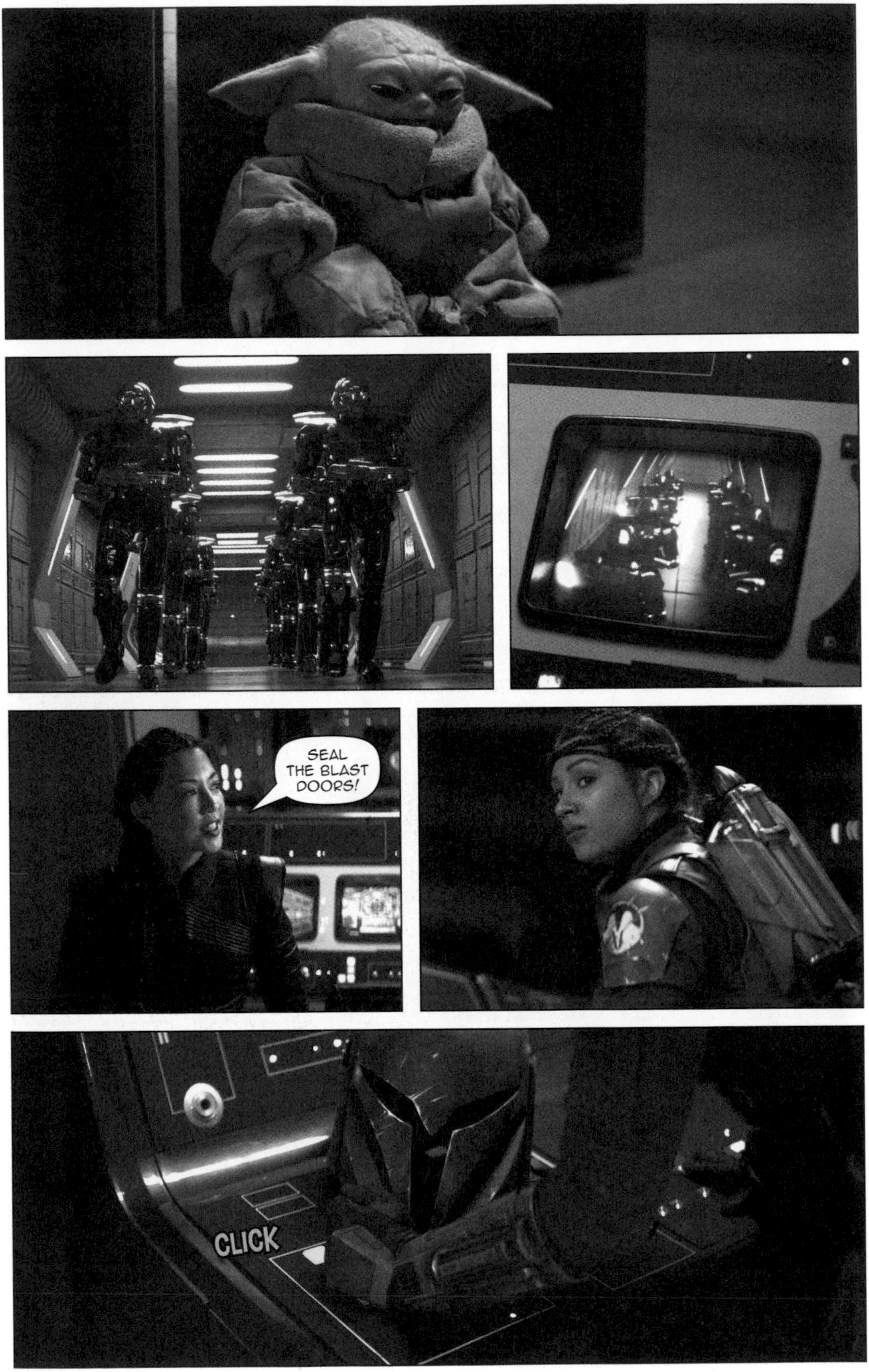
SEAL THE BLAST DOORS!
CLICK

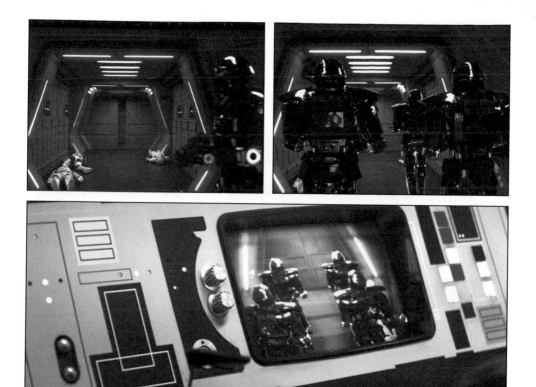

THEY'RE HERE.

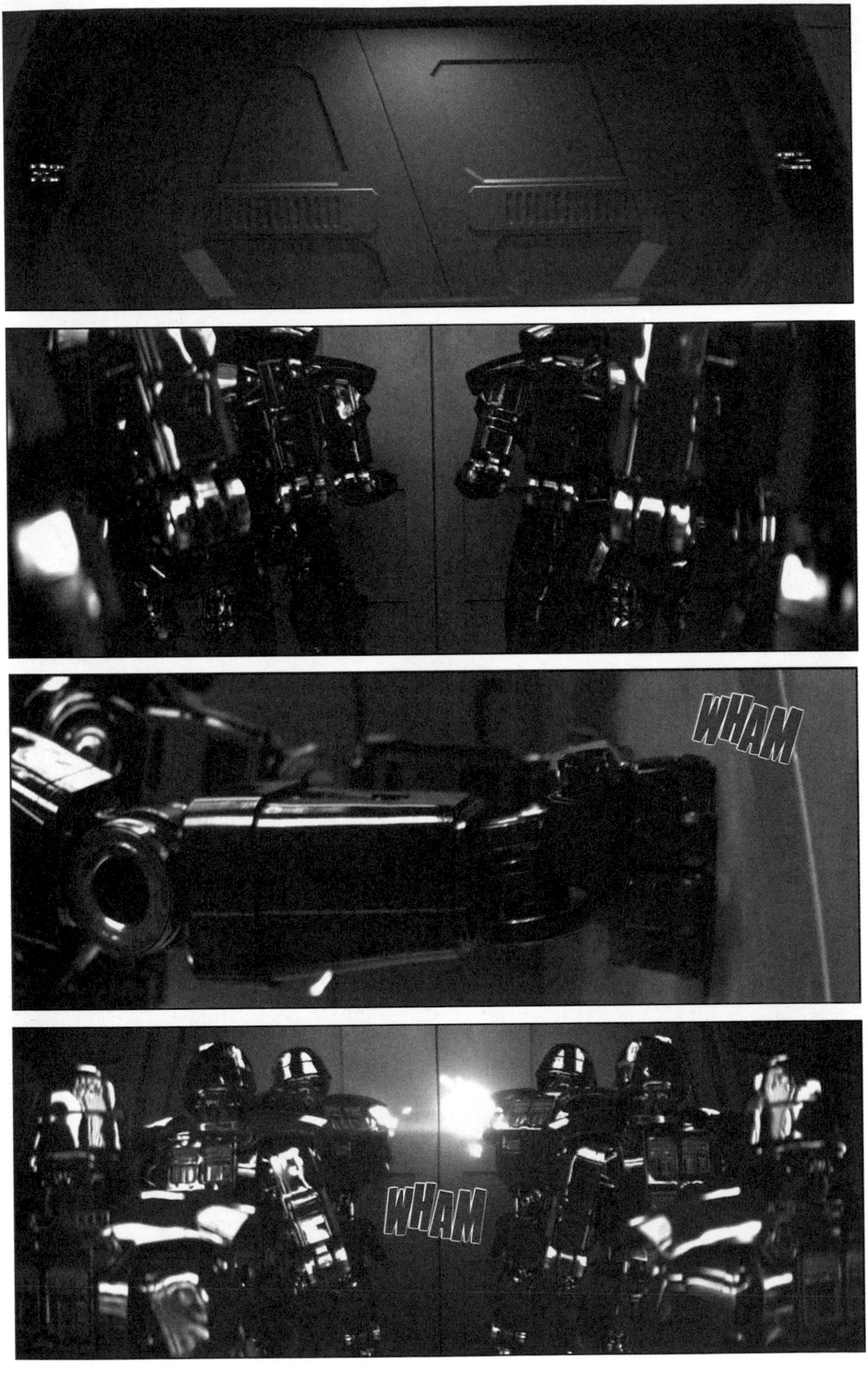
WHAM
WHAM

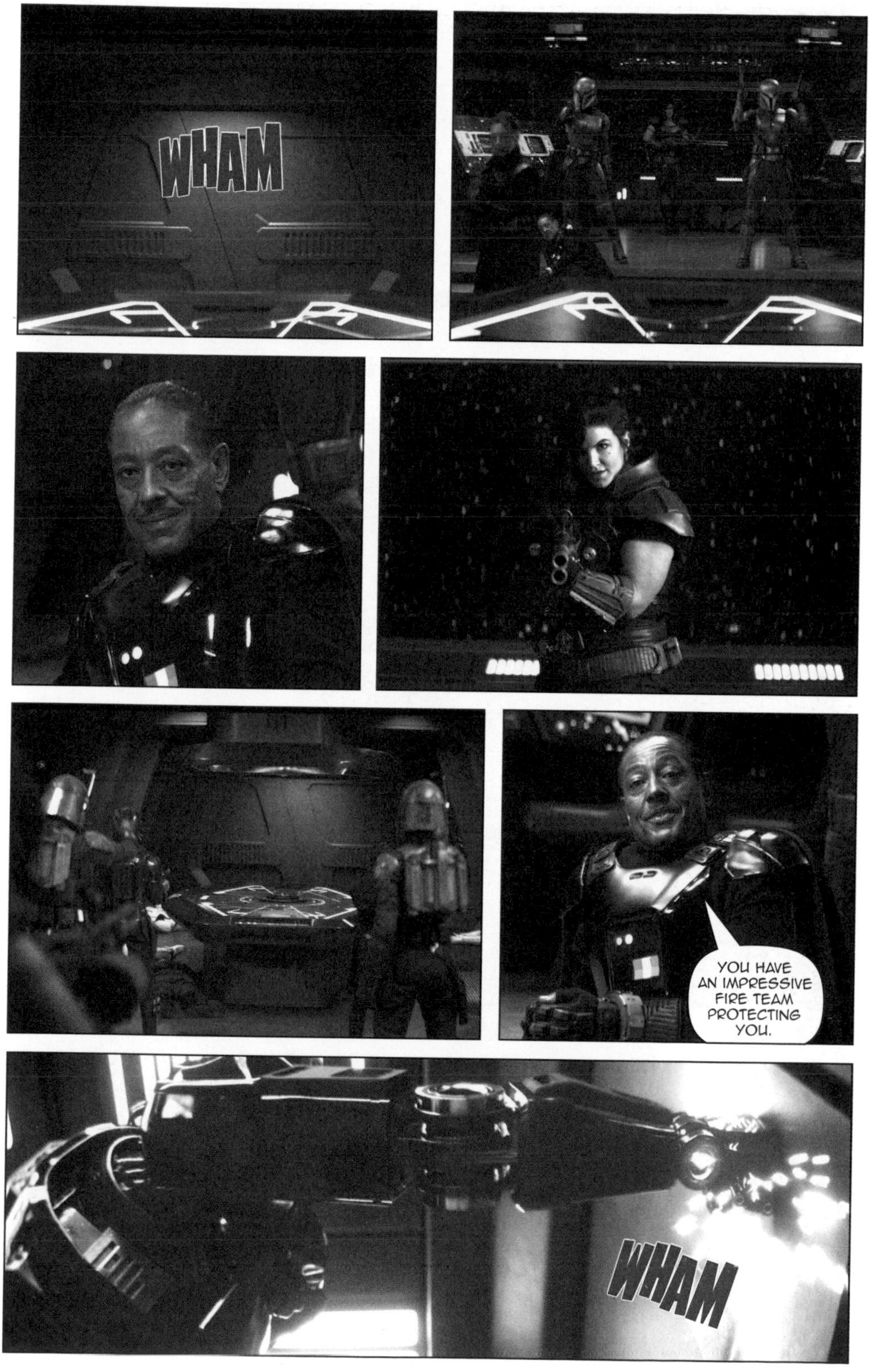
WHAM
YOU HAVE AN IMPRESSIVE FIRE TEAM PROTECTING YOU.
WHAM

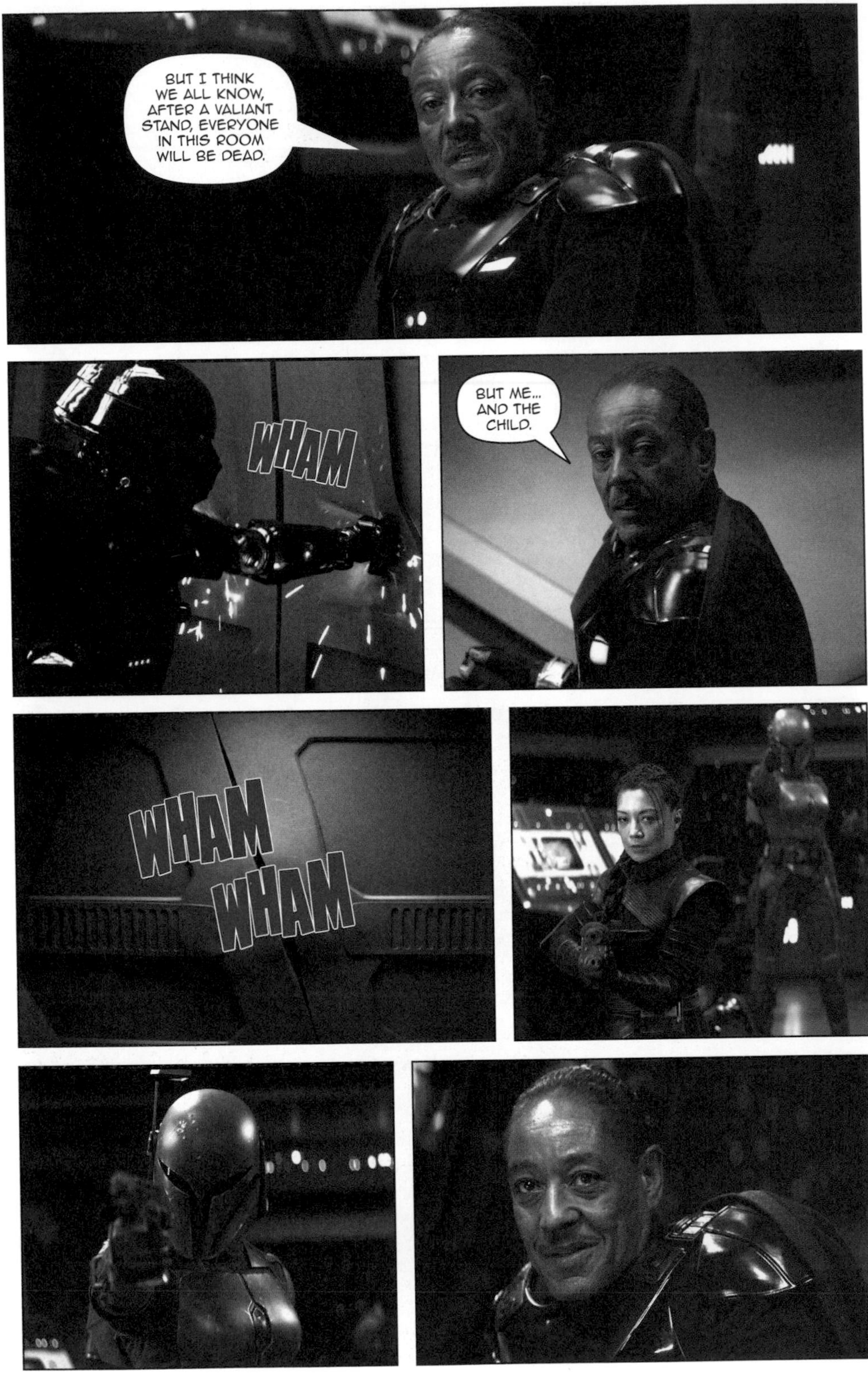
BUT I THINK WE ALL KNOW, AFTER A VALIANT STAND, EVERYONE IN THIS ROOM WILL BE DEAD.
WHAM
BUT ME... AND THE CHILD.
WHAM
WHAM

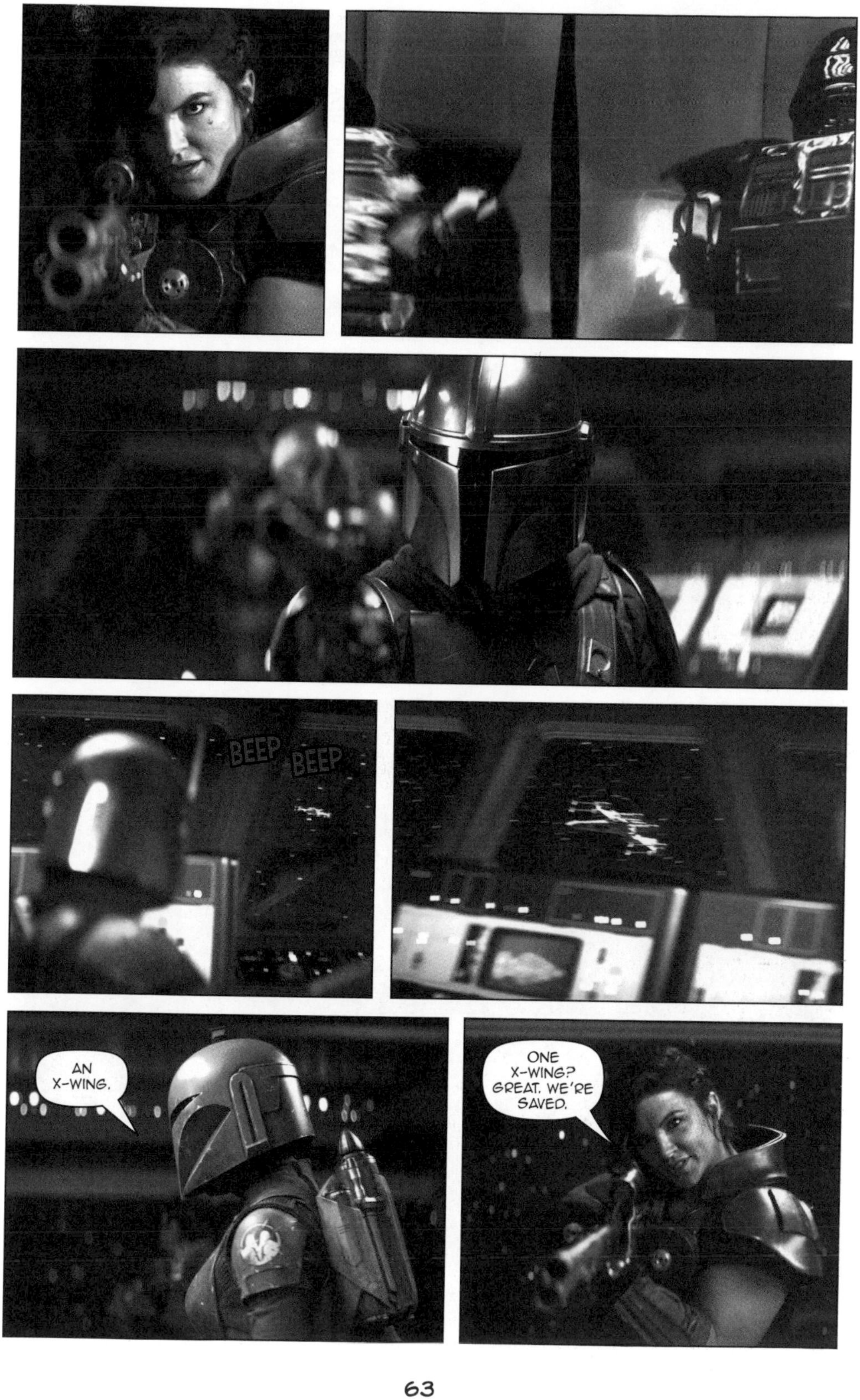
BEEP
BEEP
AN X-WING.
ONE X-WING? GREAT. WE'RE SAVED.

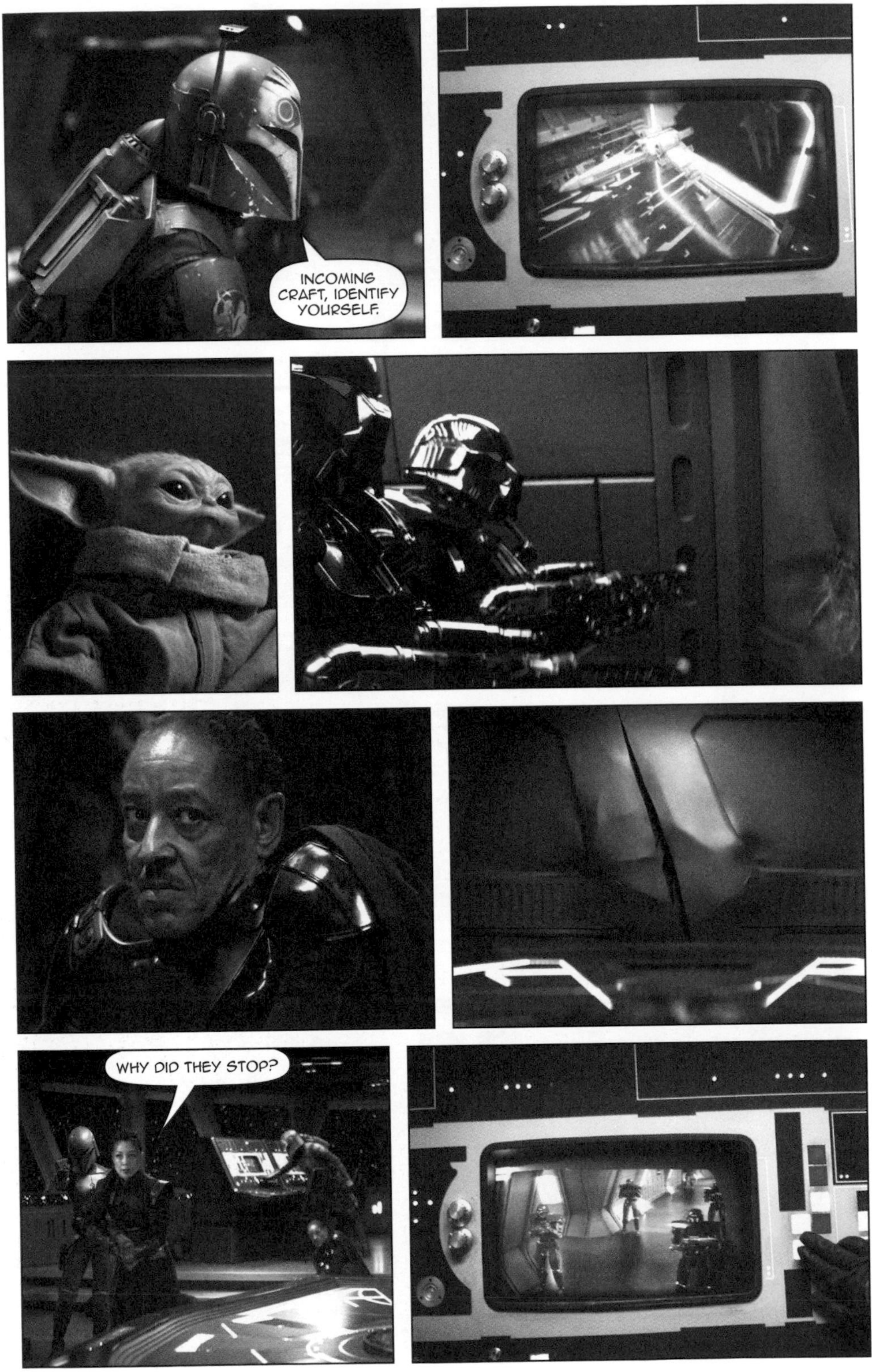
INCOMING CRAFT, IDENTIFY YOURSELF.
WHY DID THEY STOP?

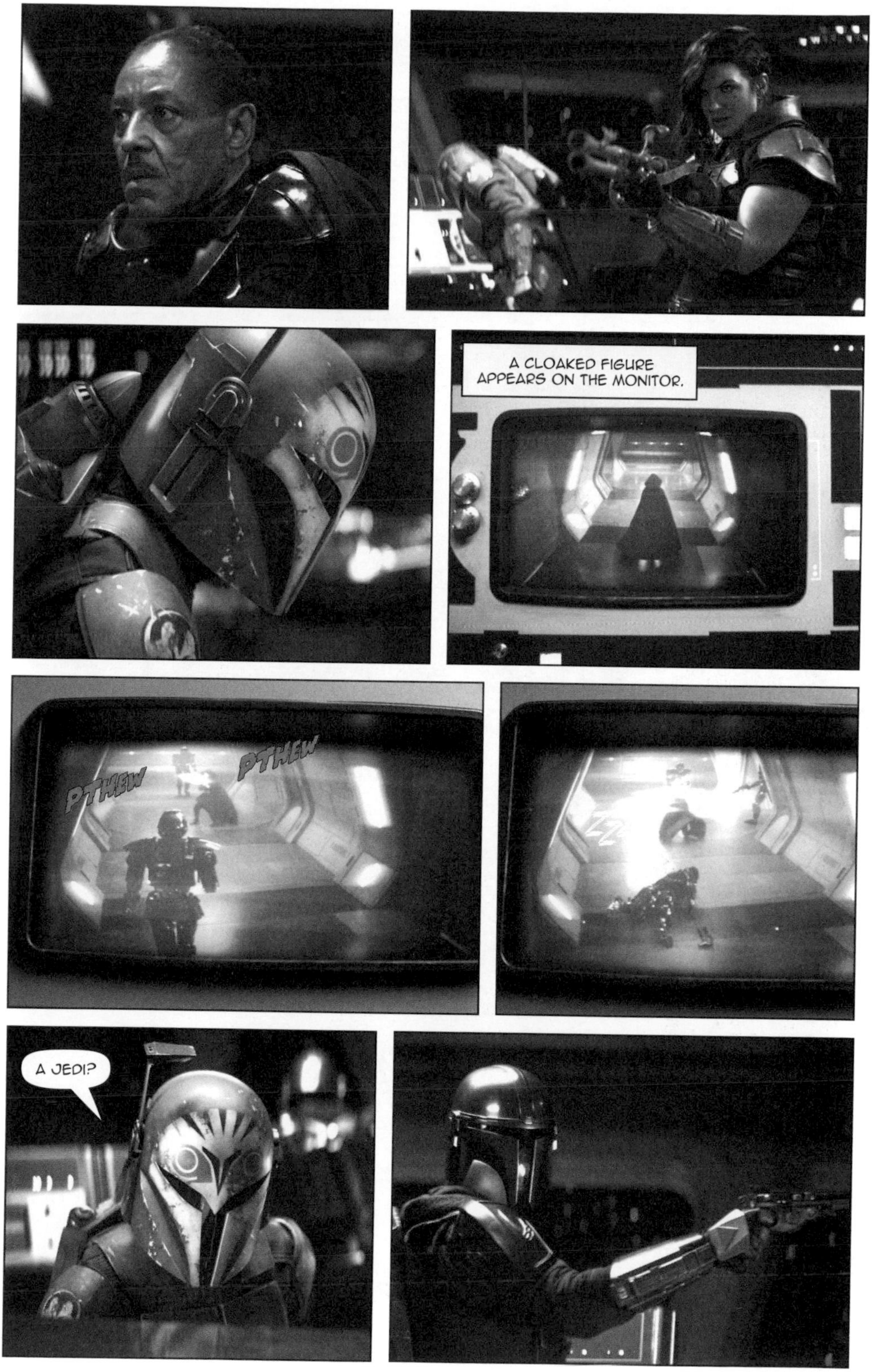
A CLOAKED FIGURE APPEARS ON THE MONITOR.
PTHEW
PTHEW
A JEDI?

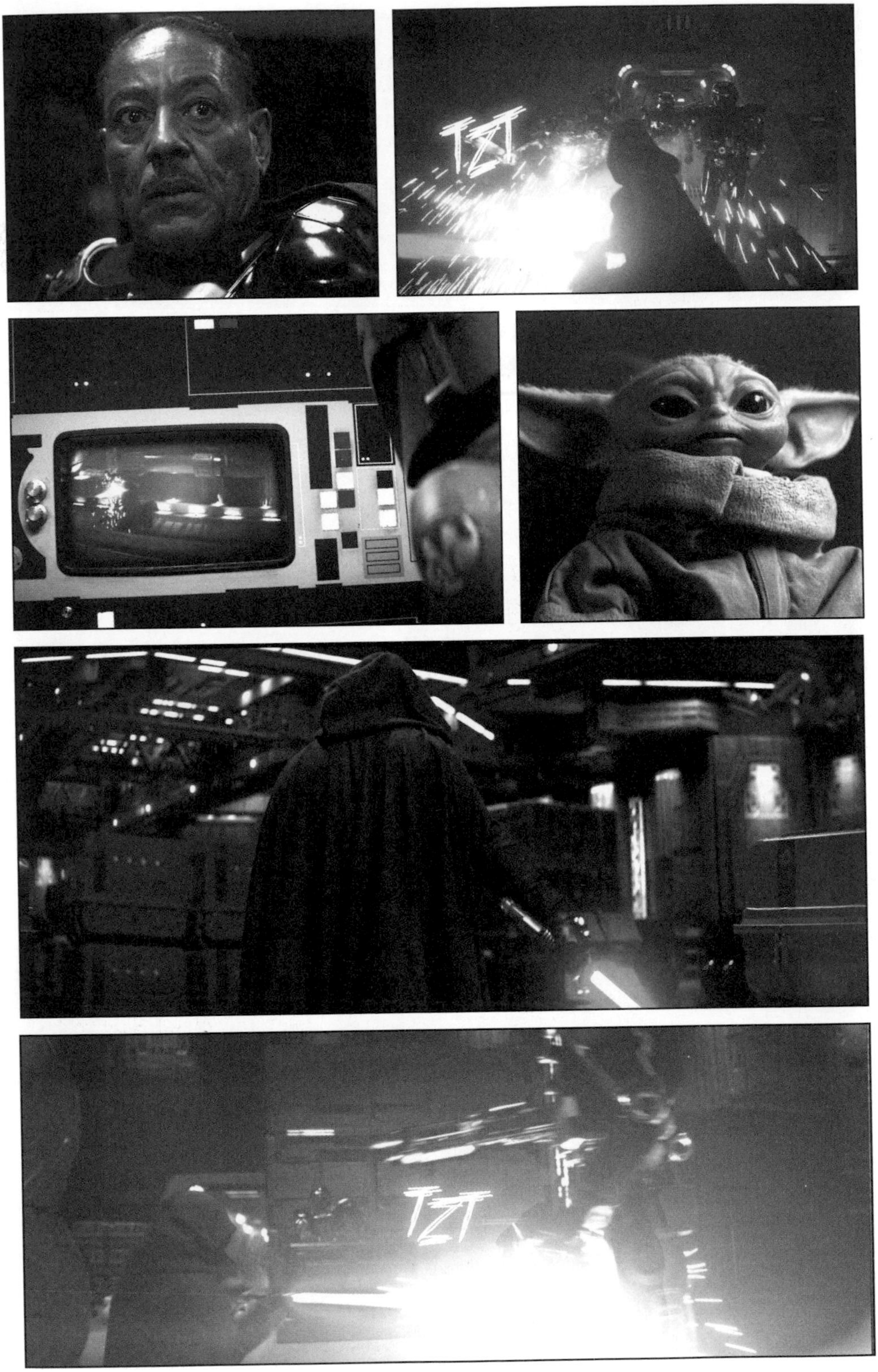

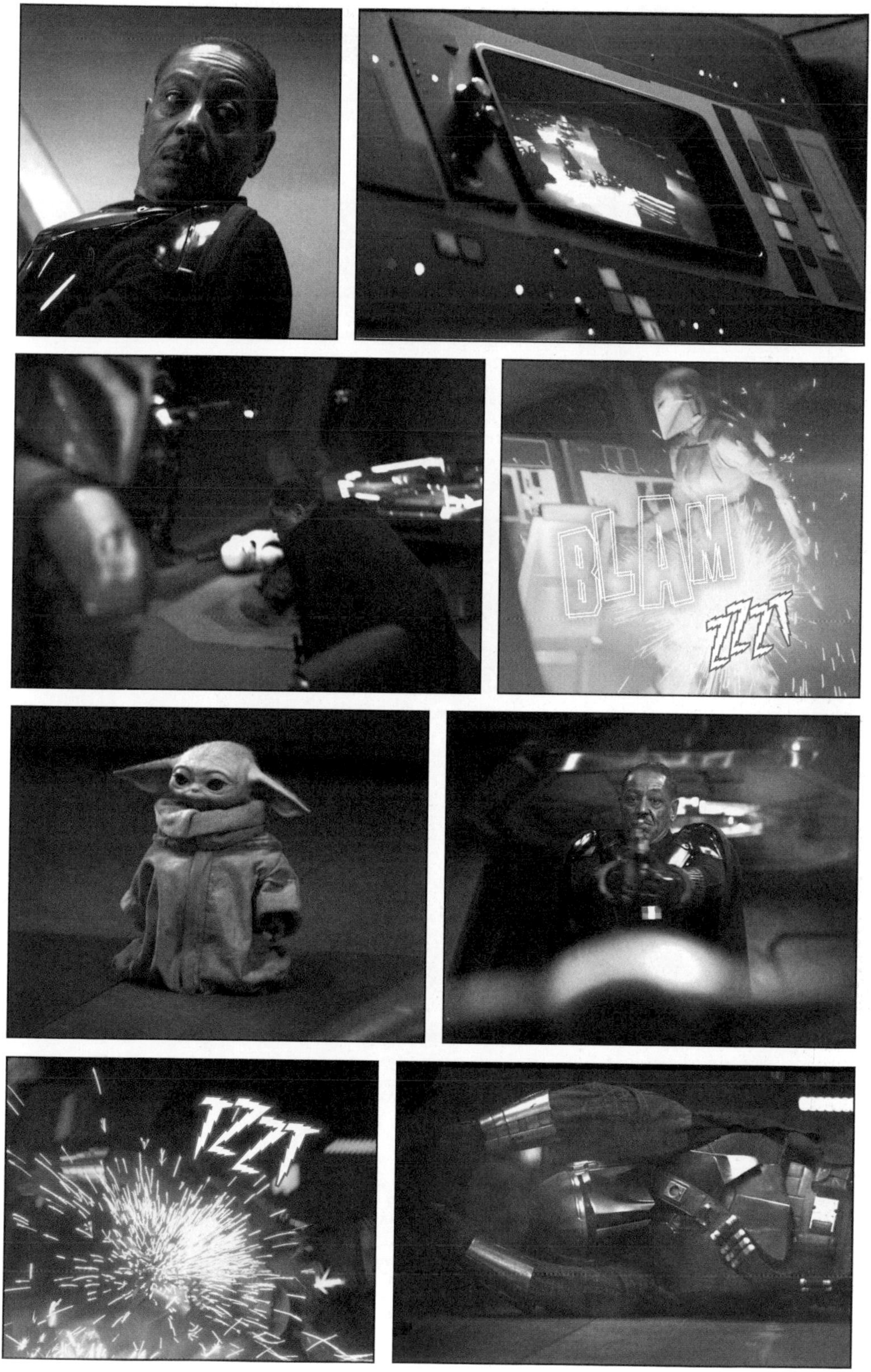
BLAM
TZZT
TZZT

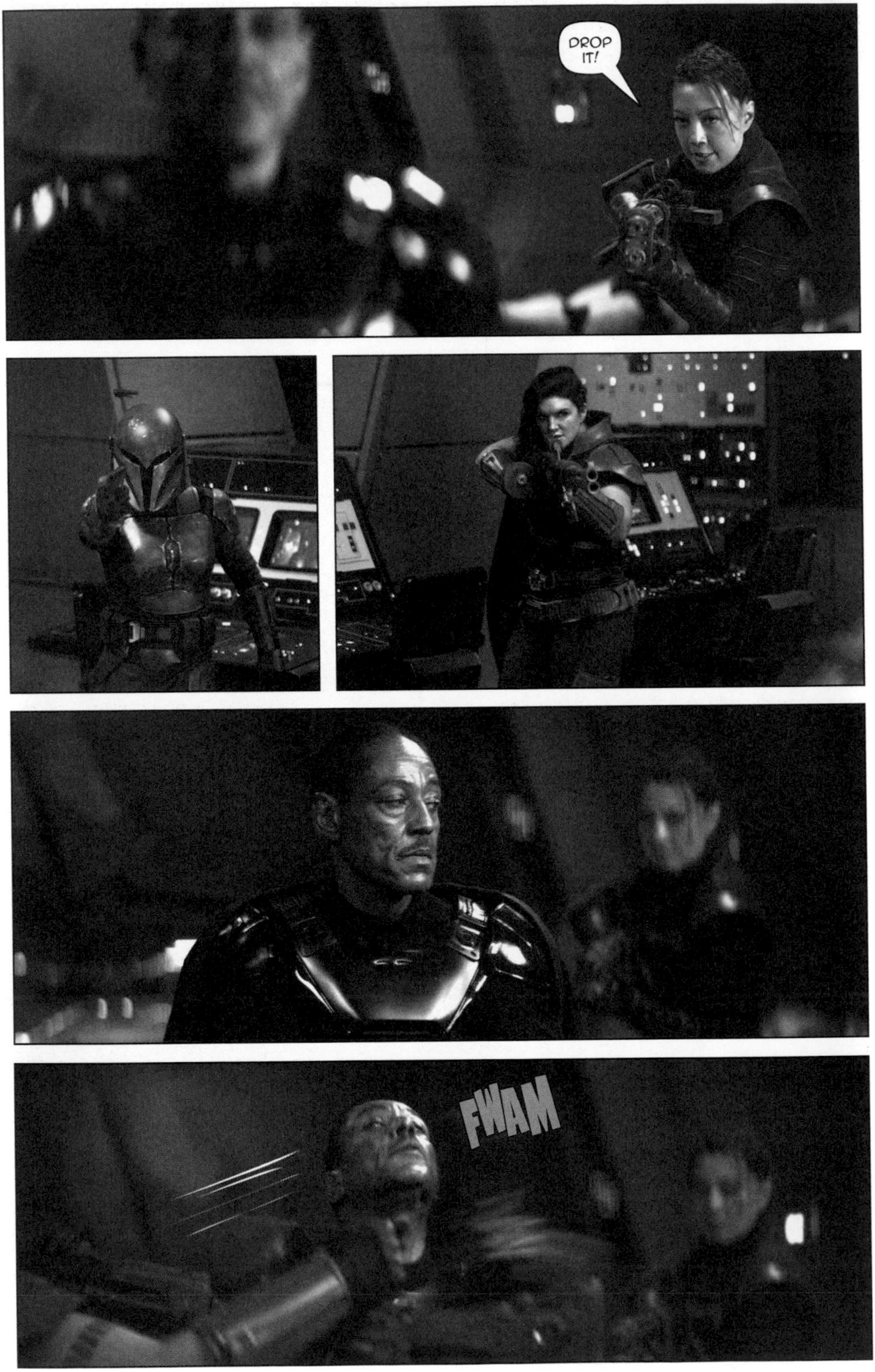
DROP IT!
FWAM

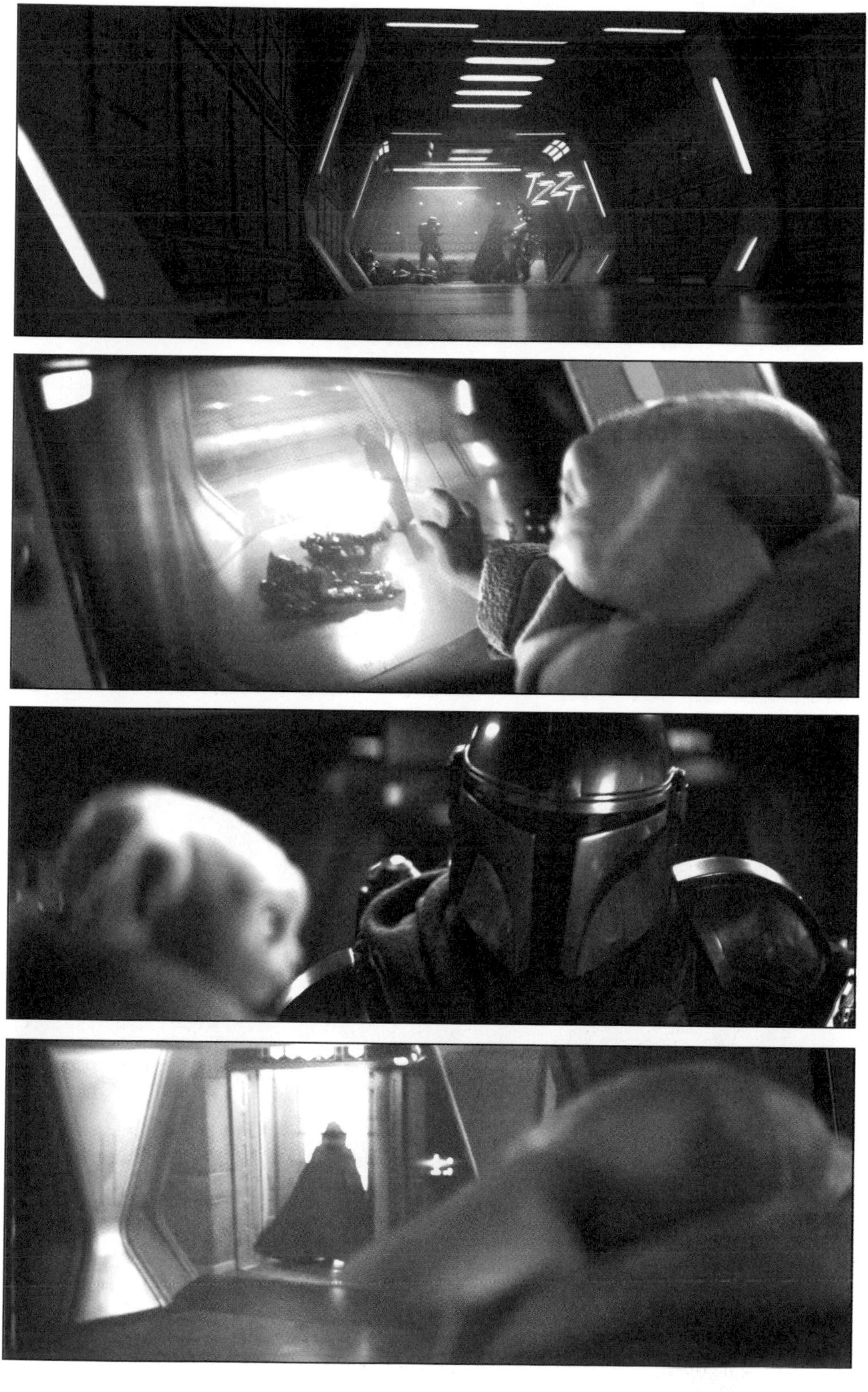
TZZT

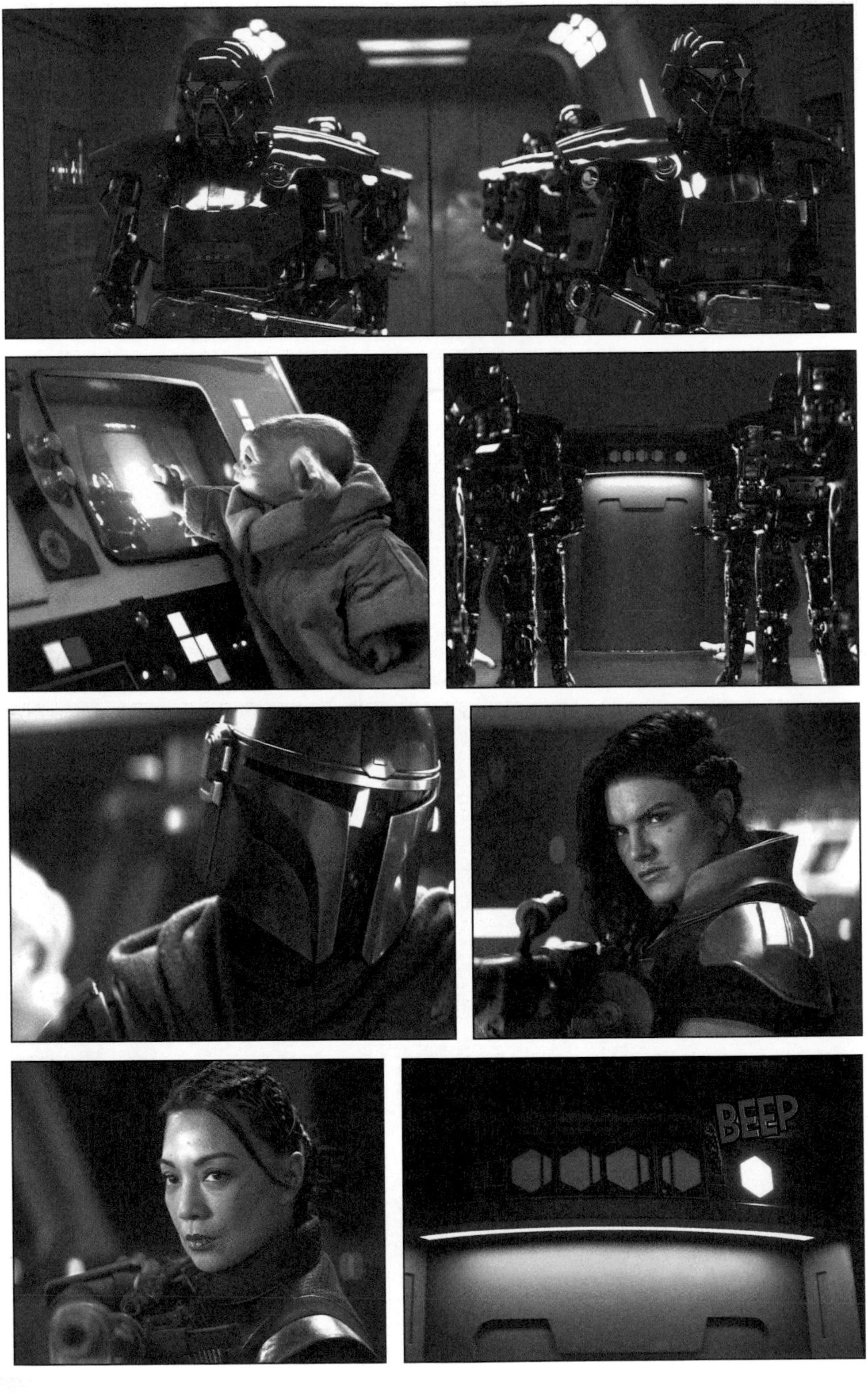
BEEP

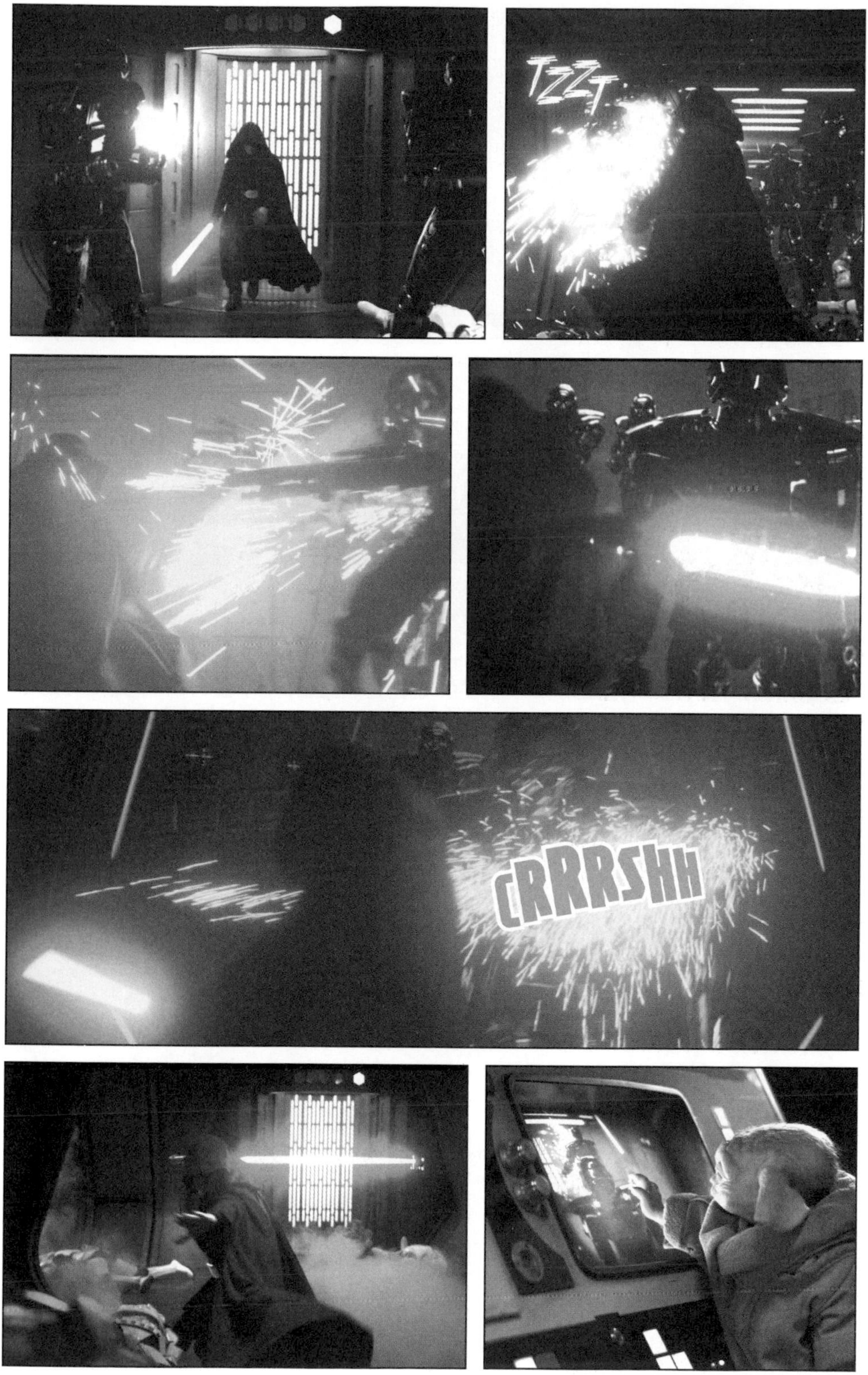
TZZT
CRRRSHH

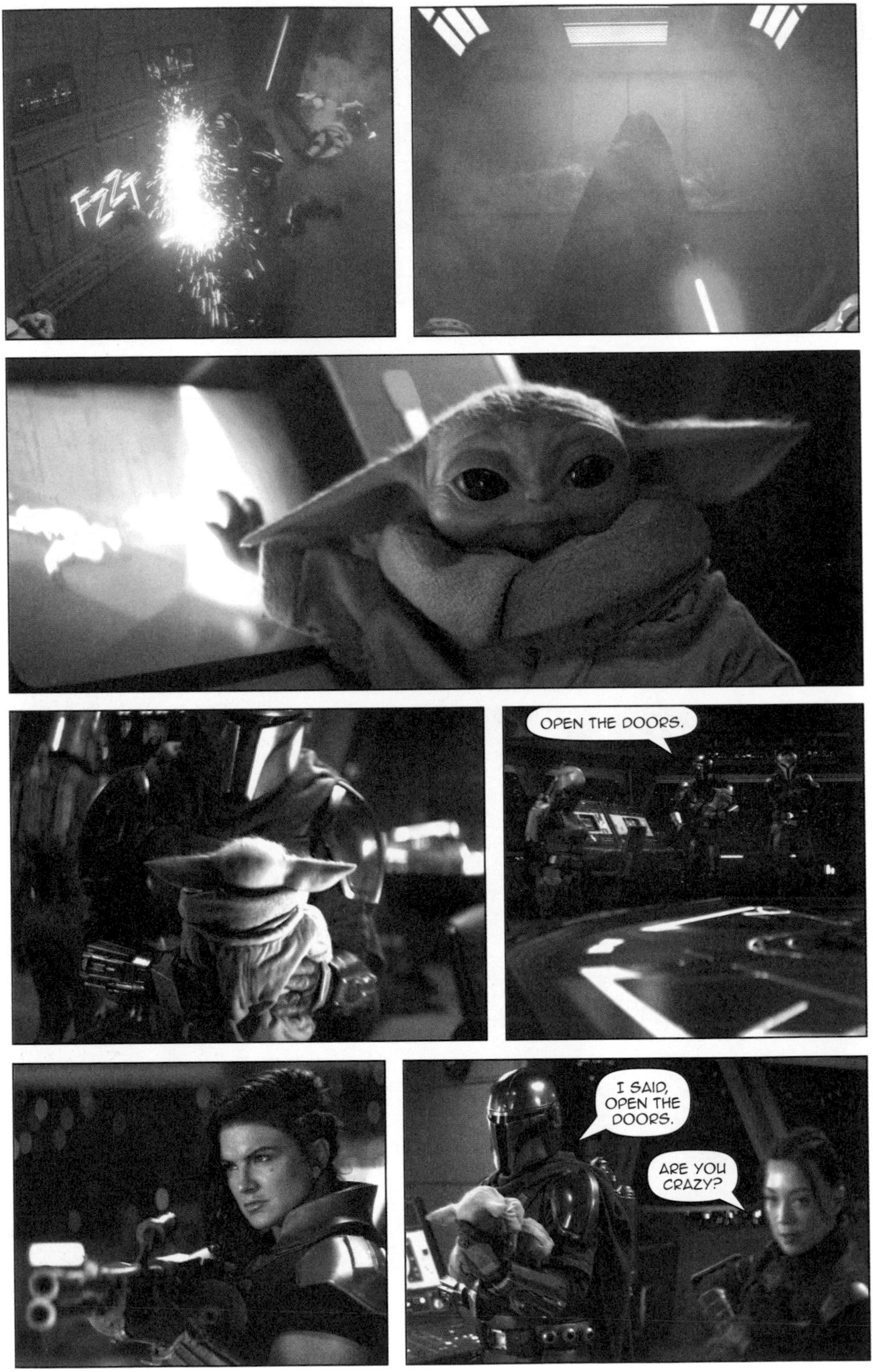
FZZT
OPEN THE DOORS.
I SAID, OPEN THE DOORS.
ARE YOU CRAZY?

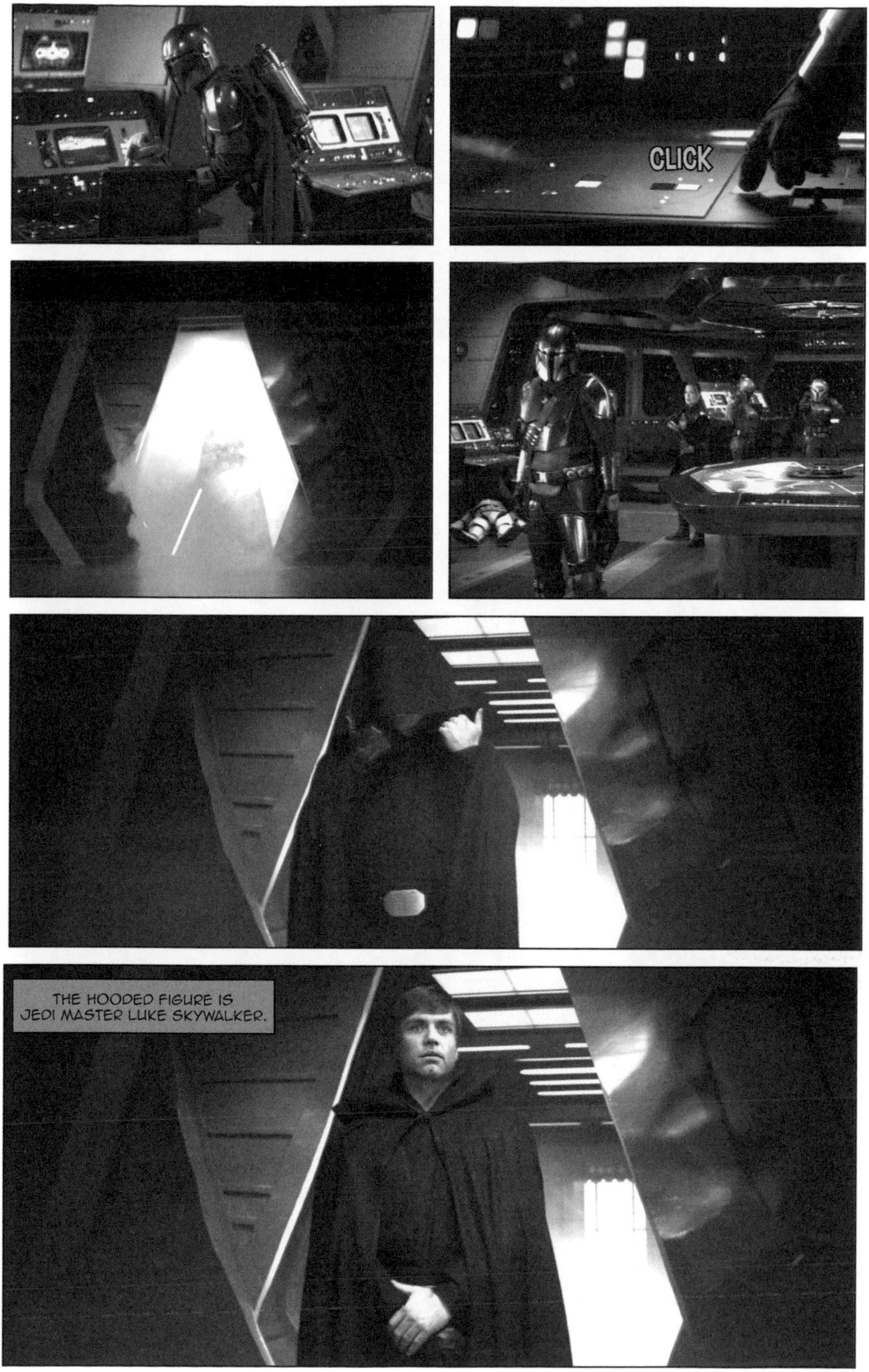
CLICK
THE HOODED FIGURE IS JEDI MASTER LUKE SKYWALKER.

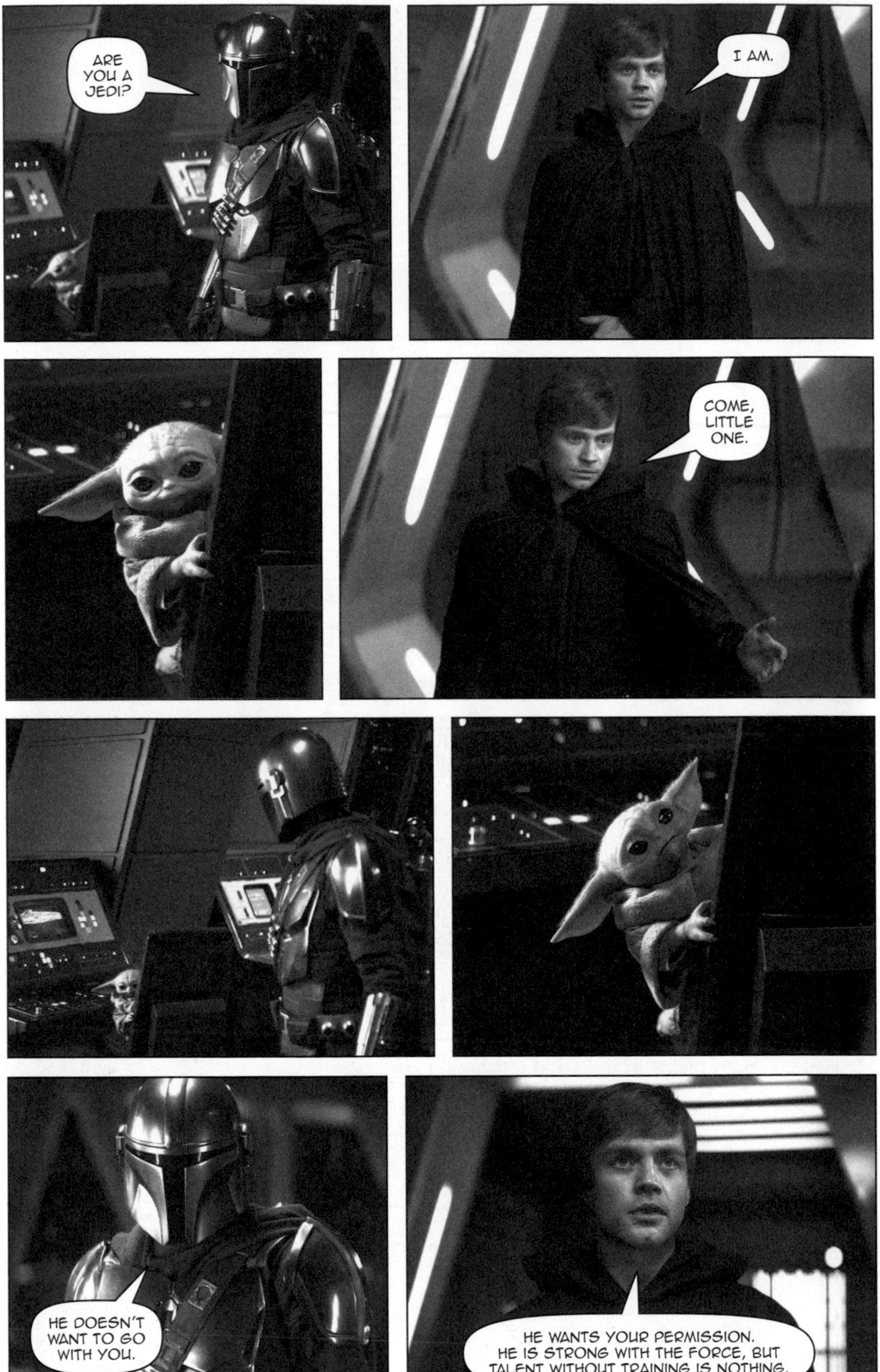
ARE YOU A JEDI?
I AM.
COME, LITTLE ONE.
HE DOESN'T WANT TO GO WITH YOU.
HE WANTS YOUR PERMISSION. HE IS STRONG WITH THE FORCE, BUT TALENT WITHOUT TRAINING IS NOTHING.

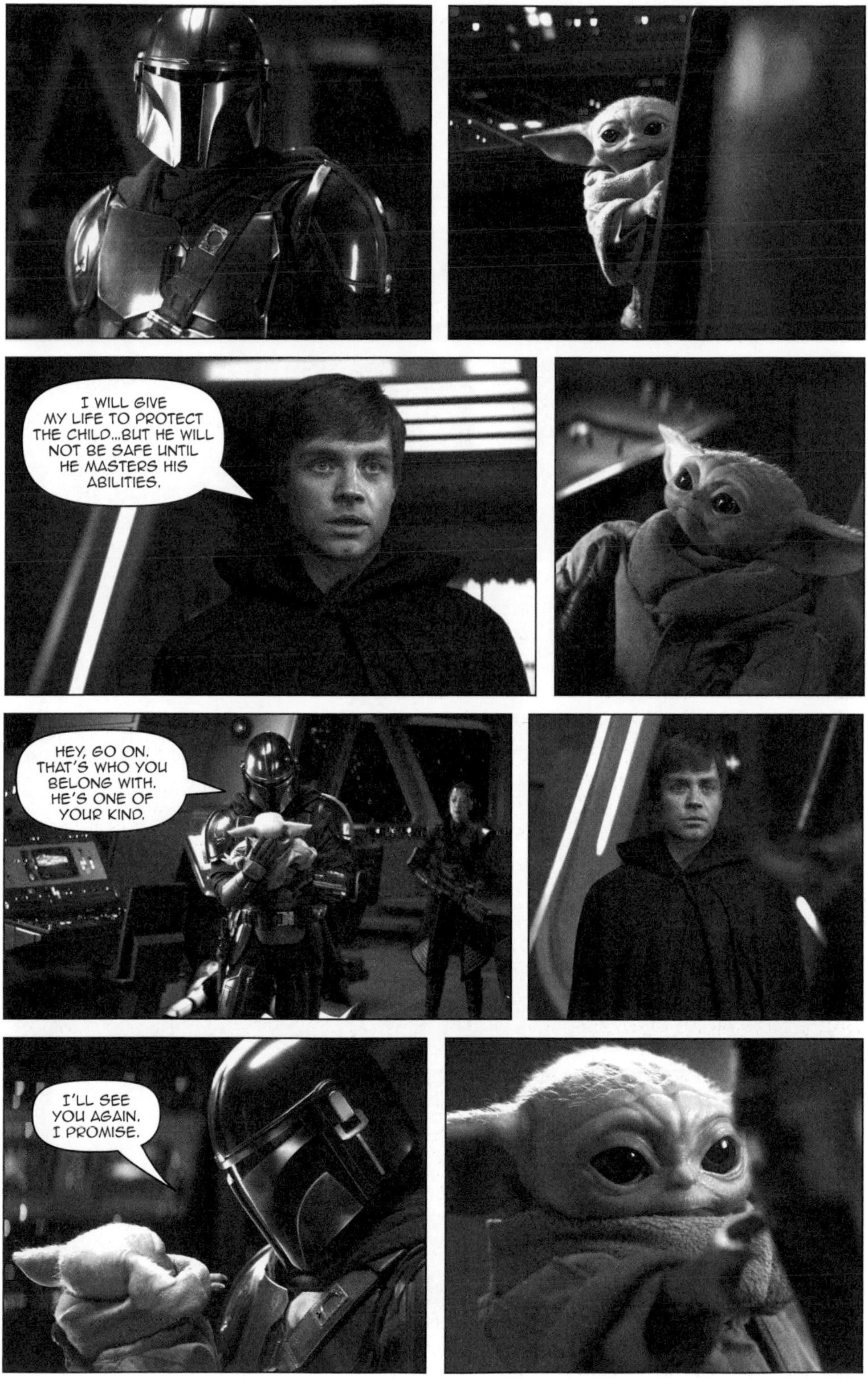
I WILL GIVE MY LIFE TO PROTECT THE CHILD...BUT HE WILL NOT BE SAFE UNTIL HE MASTERS HIS ABILITIES.
HEY, GO ON. THAT'S WHO YOU BELONG WITH. HE'S ONE OF YOUR KIND.
I'LL SEE YOU AGAIN. I PROMISE.

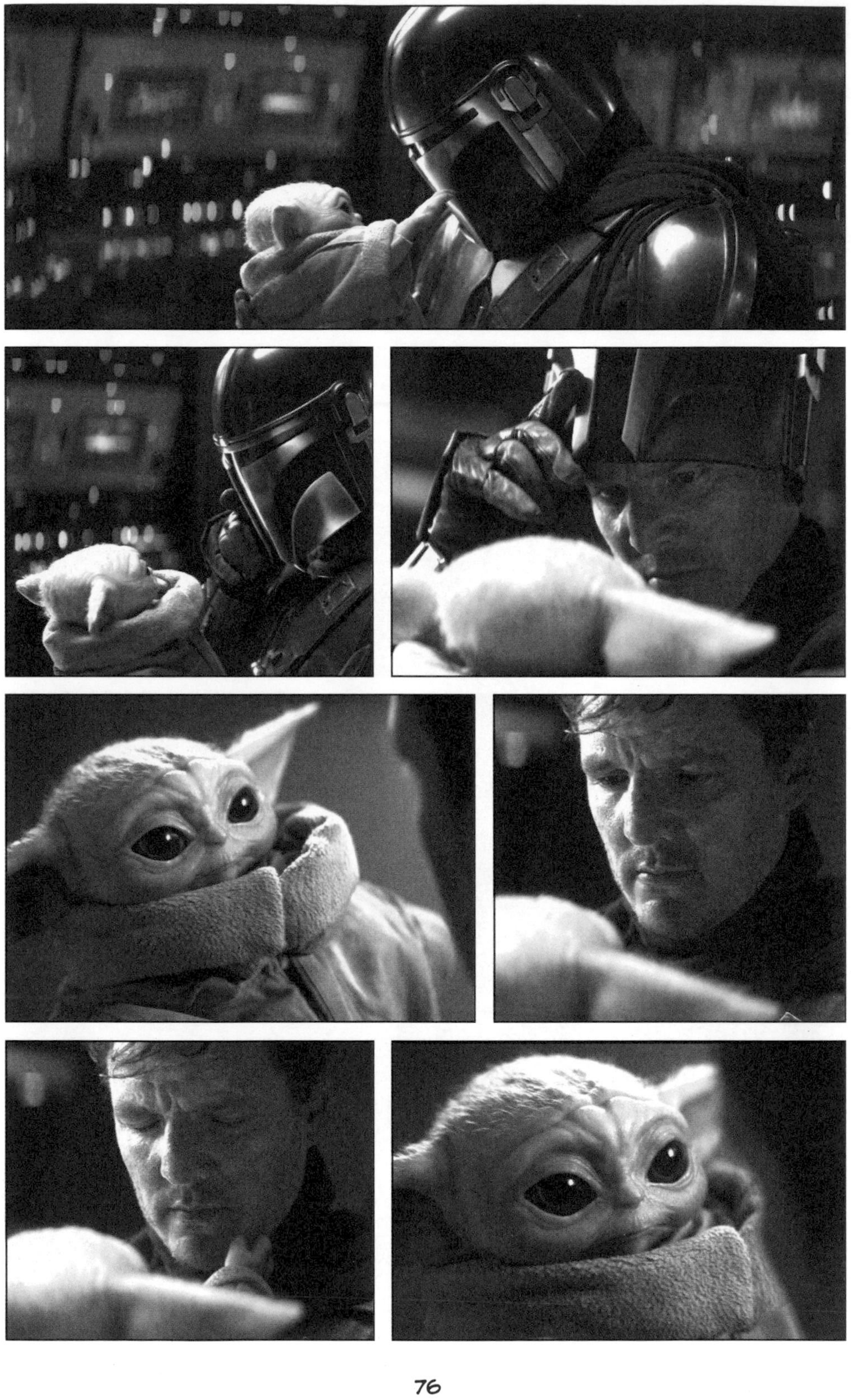

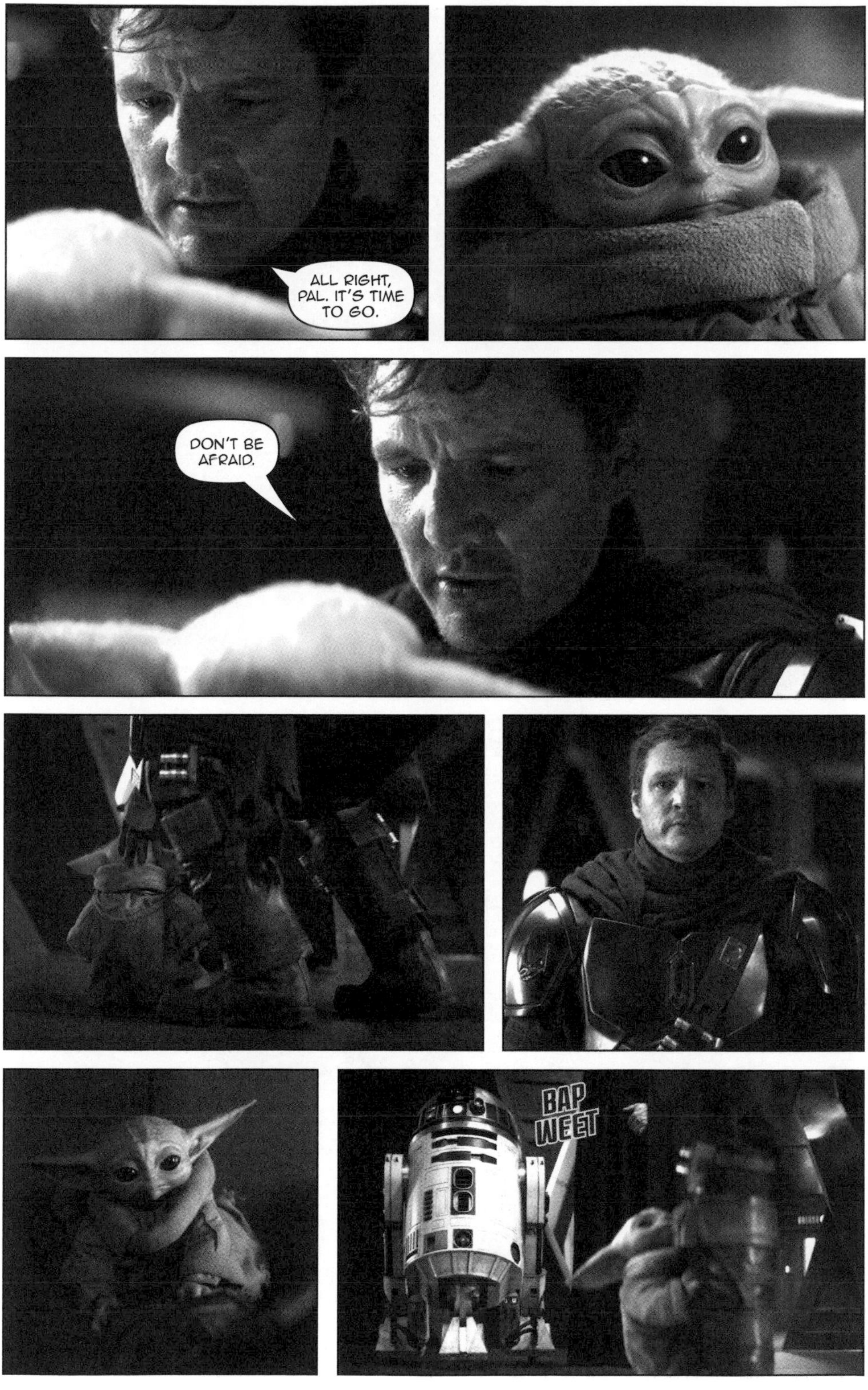
ALL RIGHT, PAL. IT'S TIME TO GO.
DON'T BE AFRAID.
BAP WEET

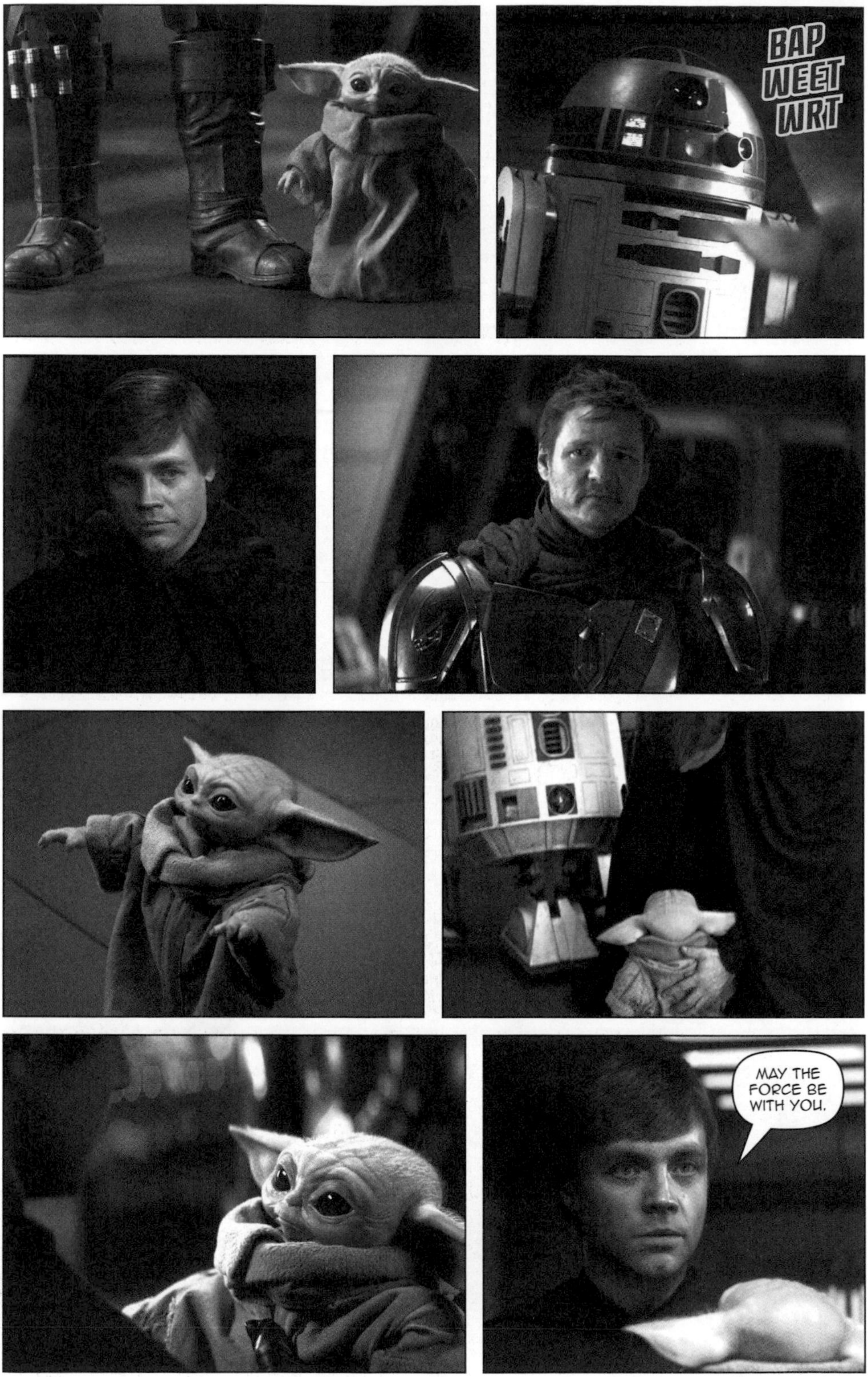
BAP
WEET
WRT
MAY THE FORCE BE WITH YOU.

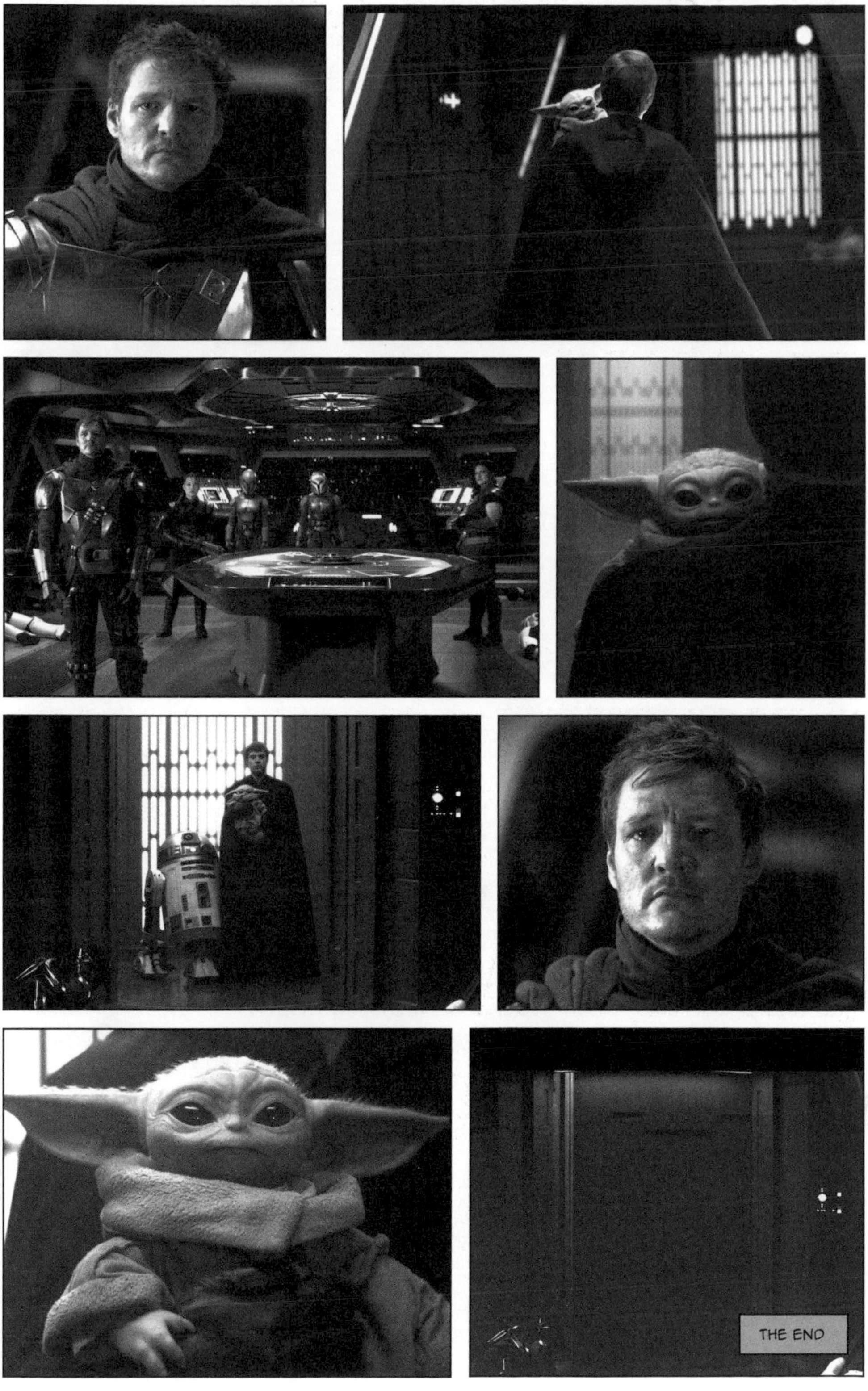
THE END

STAR WARS

THE

MANDALORIAN

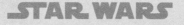

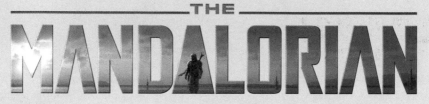

Executive Producers

Jon Favreau

Dave Filoni

Kathleen Kennedy

Colin Wilson

Directed by

Peyton Reed

Written by

Jon Favreau

For Lucasfilm

Senior Editor: Robert Simpson

Creative Director: Michael Siglain

Art Director: Troy Alders

Project Manager, Digital & Video Assets: LeAndre Thomas

Creative Art Manager: Phil Szostak

Lucasfilm Story Group: Pablo Hidalgo, Matt Martin, and Emily Shkoukani